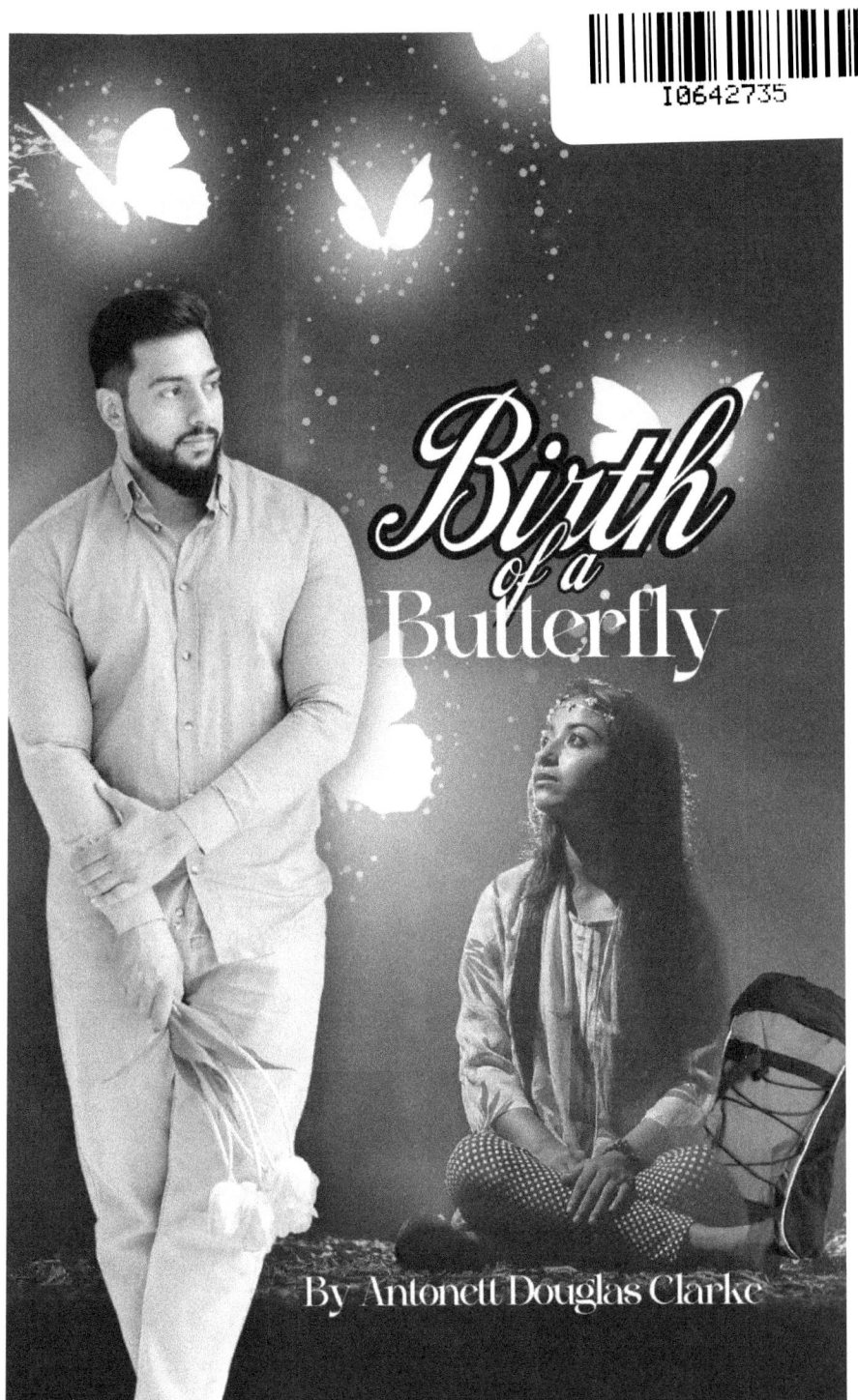

Birth of a Butterfly

By Antonett Douglas Clarke

The Birth

of a

Butterfly

Antonett Douglas Clarke

Printed in the United States of America.

Book Design, ISBN# and Formatted by Barnett Publishing

CHAPTER ONE

As soon as she finished her ten-hour shift, she ran swiftly to her locker room and removed her coffee-stained uniform. She shook her head sorrowfully as she stared at the coffee stains and then at her purse that only had five dollars. There was no way she could use the laundromat, and this was one of her two best uniforms. She had to throw out the others because they all got ruined and now, she was down to two, one of which was now stained with coffee. She knew she could not ask her supervisor for another set of uniforms because when she started her job as a housekeeper, she was given three uniforms for free but after that, any additional uniforms came at a cost she could not afford now. She sighed deeply as she stuffed her stained uniform in a plastic bag and changed into her casual clothes.

"Hey, Tapatio!" This was the nickname her co-workers gave her after an incident which happened a few months ago. Since then, she had been stuck with that name. She closed her locker when her co-worker, Marge, entered the room. Marge was twice her age but proved to be a loyal friend to her. She was somewhat like a mother to her. "It was a busy day, right kiddo?" "Yes, it was," Sequoia said facing Marge.

"I hope that school thing comes through for you soon, darling. This place is getting uglier by the minute and a beautiful young girl like yourself should not have to be treated like that. Leave it for me and the other old geezers to bear." Marge gave Sequoia a stern look. Marge was always encouraging her to leave her job here at Zenith Capital Industries and find something 'more age-appropriate for herself' — that was how Marge put it. Sequoia thought that it probably had something to do with the fact that most of the people who worked there as unskilled laborers were in their late forties to sixties.

When she had just started working there, several of her co-workers were always curious as to why a young lady like herself was working in that job capacity. But Sequoia made it clear that she was only working at Zenith Capital Industries until she saved enough money for college. However, this was a lie she told them, so they could stop questioning her. Yes, she had in fact planned to go to college but that was not going to happen for a long while. She did not even have a high school diploma—well a legit one, that is, but she kept that information to herself. Also, she was never able to save whenever she got paid. All her funds went back into her cost of living, which was sadly not much. In addition, she had a huge credit card debt to pay; a significant amount of her salary went towards that.

"Marge, you know I don't plan to stay here forever," she managed to say as she faked a smile. "I know, I know. I just cannot help myself sometimes when I see how they treat you. Especially that witch Ashley Cunningham... God she is such a bitch! Sequoia laughed. Ashley was the assistant manager of the company. She always belittled those who worked in a lower class than herself, but she especially always intentionally provoked Sequoia. For some strange reason Ashley hated Sequoia and Marge thought it was because Sequoia was much more beautiful and attractive than her. Sequoia always dismissed that rationale because she always doubted herself and her beauty that people often complimented. In her eyes, she was just five feet five inches tall, West Indian with dark skin and a petite body.

"I have found ways to cope with her bitchiness. I have better things to worry about than her." Marge shook her head saying, "That is what I love about you. You never let people get to you; you always find a way." She returned her smile and picked up her purse. "See you tomorrow." "Bye!" And with that, she left the room. After an hour and a half bus ride, she reached home and made her way inside. In the living room, she saw Stacey and her two kids watching television. She sighed deeply as she found the courage to get Stacey's attention. She slowly peered from behind the wall until Stacey realized her presence and approached her.

Stacey silently gestured for her to go towards the kitchen. "How was work?" Sequoia asked. "It was good, nothing out of the ordinary. What is up with you?" Stacey had a stern look as Sequoia tried to muster up the courage to speak. "Um... nothing much, you know, just the same old, same old." Stacey sighed and asked, "What do you want, Sasha? I know you did not call me here to ask about my day."

Sasha was the name Stacey called Sequoia because somehow, deep down she did not trust her fully from the day they met. "Fine, it's this." Sequoia took her stained uniform from the plastic bag and showed Stacey. "I know we talked about this and..." Stacey frowned and cut her off, "No, No, Sasha! You know we have a rule. Do not come and give me that bullshit." She lowered her voice as she glanced towards the living room and back before closing the kitchen door.

"Please, Stacey, I only have two uniforms and I can't afford the laundromat right now or else I won't have enough funds to get to work tomorrow." "And what am I supposed to do about that! Huh?? You know that I am the only one working and paying the mortgage and bills. The electrical bill was almost three hundred dollars last week and I had to find every cent to pay it all by myself. I cannot afford to use electricity to just wash one piece of clothing! I am sorry but that is how it is." "It would not be one piece of clothing, as you could add a few more clothes from your laundry. Please, it's just this one time." "I said no! I am already doing enough for you by having a stranger living in one of my garages." "Really, Stacey? A stranger?" Sequoia scoffed.

"Yes, a stranger because last time I checked, I never knew you two years ago, and I certainly still do not know you! We are not family. So, I think I have been kind enough to you. I am sorry but I cannot help you. Now, if you will excuse me, I must go back to spending time with my kids. Please, see yourself out of my kitchen." Stacey stormed out of the kitchen and left Sequoia dumb founded, slowly making her way to the door that led to the garage. Several thoughts crossed her mind as she made her way to her bed. Normally, she budgeted to use the laundromat every two weeks and interchange between wearing her two uniforms for the five days of work each week without getting them soiled, but sometimes the unplanned happened. It was like trying to quickly drink a cup of coffee before your supervisor come looking for you.

She inhaled deeply as she sat at the edge of her bed looking around the small room, with tears running down her face. How did she get here? She thought to herself. There she was, sitting in someone's garage where she had lived for two years because she had nowhere else to go. The good thing was the space was big enough for her to put some of her stuff in. She had a couple of baskets full of her clothes around, a small dresser with a mirror, a microwave, a small refrigerator, and a couple of garbage bags lying around with a bunch of her other personal items.

She felt a nice hot shower would help ease her tension headache, but as part of Stacey's rule, she could only shower at night, when the children were asleep. It felt like torture living there but she had no choice. She wiped her tears, went over to her small fridge for a half-eaten sandwich and a coke, and then sat on her little bean bag wallowing in her emotions. She took a photograph of herself and her mother from her purse and stared at it heartbroken. Her life had changed a lot after her mother died. It was the lowest point in her life, but it also made her who she was — a survivor. Her dreams of moving from the West Indies to America with her mother for a better future became a nightmare she would never forget. Eventually, she pushed her thoughts aside and fell into a deep sleep.

In her dreams, there she was, standing by a water fountain. It was not just any water fountain, but the wishing kind. In her palm was a quarter which she threw in the fountain with her eyes closed, as she made a wish. When her eyes opened, she locked eyes with a familiar face on the other side of the fountain. "Mom?" She ran around the fountain to see her mother dressed in red, holding a chrysalis in the palm of her hands. When Sequoia went closer, she saw that a butterfly was struggling to free itself of the chrysalis.

"My baby, you have grown so much," she hugged her tightly not wanting to let go. "I miss you so much! I feel like such a failure without you," she cried heavily in her arms. "A failure? You are my child... you are strong. Never forget that. Even at your lowest, there is still time for a miracle." As she spoke, she stroked the chrysalis and miraculously, the butterfly broke free and flew out gracefully into the blue sky.

"But..." "Do not give up my daughter, as struggle and criticism are the prerequisite for greatness." Before she could respond, she was suddenly awakened by her cellphone's vibration. She then rubbed her eyes and looked at the screen. It was an email from the credit card company, reminding her of her due payment for her over limit credit card. She groaned in frustration as she pushed her phone under the pillow.

CHAPTER TWO

As soon as Sequoia arrived at work, she made her way to the locker room and changed into her uniform. She had spent a couple of hours in the bathroom last night using some of the shower gel and her rag to remove the stain. It did not look noticeable; only a small stubborn spot remained on the waist area, so she wore her orange fanny pack that complemented the color of her uniform to cover it up.

Sequoia hummed to herself as she cleaned the staff bathroom. She was almost finished when she heard stilettos echoing in the distance as it came closer; she knew exactly who it was. As expected, Ashley appeared through the door and walked past her as if she did not exist. She even almost knocked down the wet floor sign. She entered the bathroom stall and was out in a few minutes.

"That toilet is blocked and needs some plunging. I cannot have my staff using that hideous thing." She gave Sequoia a sinister smile as she washed her hands. Before she left the bathroom, she kicked over a bucket of water, soaking the whole floor. "Oops! I am such a klutz, get that cleaned up will you," she winked and left a disgruntled Sequoia. "Oh my God! The nerve of this lady. I am so tired of her treating me like this. Ever since I stood up to her some months ago, she has made my life a living hell," Sequoia muttered to herself as she started mopping up the floor.

After an hour and a half, she had finally finished cleaning the bathroom. After, she made her way to the cafeteria where Marge waved her over to her table. "Hey, Tapatio! Where have you been?"

"Cleaning the staff bathroom on the third floor." "Unless that bathroom has expanded since yesterday, what have you been doing for so long!?" "Let's just say Ashley happened." "Oh, you poor thing," Tessa said as she snacked on a carrot. "You need to put a rabid rat in her office, and I know exactly where we can get one," Sonya added. Everyone laughed.

"It is the truth. It is the only way she will leave you alone. She needs to pick on someone her own size." "And I bet that someone is you?" Sequoia asked jokingly. "Damn right it is me. I would straighten her out like how I did Mr. Barns in IT. Damn old coot got the nerve to tell me I work too slow. Too slow my ass." Everyone laughed. "The next day, he made several trips to the bathroom after he accidentally ingested some strong ass laxatives." "And someone accidentally flooded all the toilets on the third floor, so he had to use the bathroom on the second floor," Marge added as the laughter continued. Sonya made a running motion in her seat and then gave Marge a high five.

The laughter was contagious, and Sequoia just nodded her head as she wiped a tear from her face. "You both are savages. I will not partake in such monstrosity," Sequoia mimicked in a British accent. "I would definitely describe those poops as monstrosities. I am just glad it was old Hilda who was on bathroom duty that day. God bless her poor soul;

she called in sick after that dreadful day," Sonya concluded as the laughter slowly died down.

Sonya was also a part of the little clique they had. She was around the same age as Marge. She was an African American with a saucy mouth and she had been working there the longest. Tessa was a little older than Sequoia; she was twenty-nine. Both her and Sequoia were the babies of the group. Then lastly, there was Tiffany who was in her mid-thirties and was a hot mess. She loved to wear makeup and boss everyone around, but they did not mind. She was also funny.

"Where is Tif at?" Sequoia questioned as she took a few sips of her coke. "Probably flirting again with Sam from accounts," Sonya blurted. "No, I saw her going to the fifth floor with Cindy," Tessa added. "Did they reassign her floors? I thought she was working on the same floor as us." "Well, Cindy is her gossip buddy so maybe it was a social call." Each set of housekeepers and janitors were assigned to color-coded groups and each group was assigned to specific floors for the shift. The good thing about it was that once you were assigned to a group, it was your group for life. Sequoia felt lucky knowing she was assigned to a group where she met some wonderful people, she could call friends.

Each of them had their own unique personality. "So, are you alright, my child?" Marge asked quietly as the others indulged in their own conversations. "Yeah, I am good. Do not worry about me." Marge squeezed her hand and smiled briefly. "Marge, did you tell her we are all going to Lisa's birthday party this Saturday?" Sonya asked.

"Oh, I almost forgot. Lisa wants us all to be at her birthday party at her parent's old place in Dickinson this Saturday." Lisa worked in the office as a senior accountant. She was one of the very few people who socialized with them despite what her co-workers thought. She was different from the rest; she never once belittled others. "Dickinson? That is ninety-nine miles from here. How are we going to get there?"

"My boyfriend is going to pick us all up and take us in his SUV. It is going to be a fun road trip," Tessa said excitedly. "So, you don't have to worry about waking up early to catch the bus, Hun, as we will be picking you up right at your door," Marge added. Sequoia felt a little uneasy at Marge's comment. As far as her co-workers knew, she lived sixteen miles away in a quiet neighborhood and a decent house by herself. But she knew her friend's way too well; she had a feeling that if they came to pick her up, they would be interested to see inside her house before they departed for their destination. But she would have to decline and then it would raise suspicion. So, she had to think of a way to avoid that before Saturday.

"Well, let's get back to the old plantation, ladies!" Sonya exclaimed as she rose to her feet. Everyone followed suit. Sequoia was so exhausted after work she fell straight into her bed once she got home. She had stopped by a restaurant earlier to pick up some

Chinese food for dinner. As she was about to change her outfit, a loud knock startled her. She climbed up three short steps of stairs and opened the door to find Stacey all dressed up. "I need you to babysit the children for me. The sitter canceled at the last minute, and I have somewhere to go."

Sequoia was baffled at her request because since she had been living there, Stacey had never asked her to babysit her children, let alone talk to them. Often, when they asked who Sequoia was, Stacey would just tell them she was a house sitter. More like a 'garage sitter' Sequoia thought to herself at the time. "Stacey, it is game night tonight. I must meet my friends in an hour." "Well, it's still early so call them and tell them you cannot make it." Sequoia's eyes dilated in shock, "Really?"

"Yes really, you live here rent free and I have never asked you for anything in return. The least you can do is babysit my kids. Look, I have to go so please go to the living room now." Then she walked off in her high heels hurriedly. Sequoia's rage burned inside, but she had no choice, so she lazily made her way to the living room. "Hey kids, remember mommy's friend? Her name is Sasha. She will be your sitter tonight. Do not give her any trouble, okay?" Stacey said kissing the children's cheeks and then handed Sequoia a list. "These are the rules as well as their allergies, so follow them. I also left popcorn in the microwave for them. I will be back at midnight." A car honked in the distance, and she quickly made her way out to the front yard. Sequoia stood up staring at the thorough list in her hand then at the children — Amy was seven and Josh was ten.

She greeted them and sat on the couch beside them. "Hi, Amy and Josh. I am Sasha, mommy's friend." "The one that lives in the garage?" Josh asked. Sequoia paused for a second before nodding her head at the four bright eyes that stared at her. "But if you're mommy's friend, why do you live in the garage?" he asked. "Yeah, why don't you ever come to play or eat with us?" Amy added. Sequoia swallowed hard trying to find the right answer. "Well, I work a lot so most of the time when you're at home, I am at work and by the time I get home you're both asleep." "But why do you live down there?"

Before she could answer, the microwave went off. "Great, your popcorn is ready! I will go set it up." She dashed to the kitchen, feeling relieved. When she returned to the living room, they had forgotten all about their questions. The rest of the night went by smoothly as she bonded with the children.

CHAPTER THREE

Sequoia yawned uncontrollably as she finished the last button on her uniform. "Rough night?" Tessa asked. "Yeah, kind of. My friend asked me to babysit her two kids last night. They were a handful, and she came back at one in the morning." "Wow, no wonder you look so tired. Take it easy today." "I will try."

"Hey, Tapatio." They turned to see Tiffany entering the room. "Ashley wants you to clean her office." "What!? Why me?" "That is what I asked. I even volunteered but she blew me off. Sorry kiddo, but the lady's got a bone to pick with you." She sighed deeply as this was not the morning to work in such proximity to her. She felt drowsy and out of it.

"All the best," Tessa empathized. She hesitantly made her way to her office. She could see Ashley pacing back and forth in her office as she spoke on her phone. The office workers who sat by their desk noticed Sequoia walking towards Ashley's office door and immediately, everyone's attention was on her. Sequoia knew that all eyes were glued on her because of the epic showdown that happened between them a few months ago and stemmed the name, "Tapatio". It started out just like this, with Sequoia going into Ashley's office to clean. It felt so much like déjà vu.

She knocked on Ashley's door softly even though she could see her from the glass window. Ashley gave her the go ahead to come in. "Paul, hold on a bit please." She covered the phone's speaker with her hand and spoke. "My office feels a bit cluttered and the air smells like wet gym socks. Could you wipe down my desk and spruce it up a bit?"

Before Sequoia could reply, she went back to her phone call. Sequoia shook her head and went straight to work. The faster she finished cleaning, the sooner she could leave the office before Ashley got off the phone. She was almost finished when she accidentally tipped over a mug of coffee on a few stacks of paper.

Her heart raced as she rushed to get the stains out as soon as possible. "What the hell is wrong with you?!" Ashley exclaimed as she hung up the phone.

"I give you one simple job to do, and you mess it up. How stupid can you get! God even knows why you are still on this damn payroll!" Sequoia glanced at the office workers on the other side of the glass and as expected, they were all staring at them. The door was opened midway, so they could hear everything.
"Get the hell away from my papers and out of my office. You are making it worse, you stupid girl!"

Sequoia stood with her arms folded and gave her a disgusted look. She then turned to leave the office but decided to stop at the door. She clenched her fists and was about to do something she would regret, when she heard someone shout from across the room. "Sequoia! Do not do it. Please." It was Marge and Tessa standing at a doorway, pleading with Sequoia. "What are you waiting for standing there? I said leave!" Ashley slammed the door in her face as Sequoia bit down hard on her lip. Everyone watched as she marched out from the room.

Marge and Tessa caught up with her in the break room. "Sequoia, I knew you had every right to slap that witch, but I could not let you. I was afraid you would not be able to stop if you started," Marge said, squeezing her hand tightly.

Sequoia just bit her lip harder as she took a deep breath in. "You know Ashley would love nothing more than to have you arrested. She would use it as an opportunity to rain more terror on your life. I know it is hard but be strong my child. You will overcome all of this. Her day of reckoning is coming." "Yes, my child," Sonya entered the room and shared a worried look. "That menace will get what she deserves but don't be the one to pull that trigger." "Thanks, guys! I don't know what I would do without you all by my side."

Sequoia fought back her tears as the group hugged her. She could feel her heart and her breathing rate slow down. In her mind, she knew many people wondered why she still kept the job, but there were two reasons why she did not quit. One reason was that she loved working with her friends since they were the closest thing to a family she had. The other reason was that she did not have legit credentials to get a job elsewhere. It was through a connection from her past that she had gotten the job and was able to bypass the mandatory hiring requirements which included a criminal background check. If it were not for that confidant, she would currently be jobless and imprisoned. It was a one-time offer given to her since her complicated past had legal implications. She also had no choice but to trust that confidante to keep her past a secret, buried under a lot of lies. In a way, her confidant was like an invisible guardian angel because if it were not for him, Ashley would have fired her a long time ago.

It was finally Saturday! After what happened a few days ago with Ashley, she was really looking forward to a party to clear her mind. Stacey had gone to the park with the kids so she could safely exit the house without being questioned. She looked at her watch and right on time, a blue SUV pulled up at her feet. "Oh my God, Girl, that is your house!" Tessa exclaimed. "I need a drink before we leave. I am sure you got a wine cellar," Sonya added. "Or an open bar. Girl child, what are you waiting for to invite us in?" "I would love to but we have a party to attend, and we have Tiffany to pick up and..."

"Tif will not be mad if we are a little late. That is as long as we give her the details about that gorgeous house of yours," Tessa pressed. "And also, my grandmother is staying with me for a while. She is not doing so well so I do not think having visitors at this time will be good for her." "Sorry to hear. So, who is going to stay with her?" "My cousins from Connecticut." "Okay, we have wasted enough time. Leave the young miss alone. She can show you her entire house next time," Marge interrupted. Saved by the bell, she thought to herself as she laughed and entered the SUV. The party was not at all what they expected. They knew Tif had always boasted about Lisa's place because she visited her once, but they always thought she was exaggerating. It was a mansion located on a big property, in an almost secluded area; they all stared in amazement.

"I guess we did not overdress," Tessa said. They shook their heads in unison. There were several cars parked at the front and there were a lot of people on the outside and the balcony as well. "Um, how are we going to find Lisa to give her the presents?? I mean we have been texting and calling her for long now and still no response." "Well..." before Sequoia could answer, they heard a loud scream. It was Lisa running towards them with her arms opened wide. She looked breathtaking in her cheetah-colored suit and matching earrings. Even her hair had cheetah-colored spots. She hugged them tightly. Everyone started complimenting her at once.

"I always thought Tiffany was exaggerating about this place!" Sonya said, as she kept looking around. "And we thought it was a small party; who are all these people Lisa?!" Tessa exclaimed, checking her face in the mirror. "Do we even look that good to be here among these people?" "Guys, calm down! You all look beautiful. I must say my parents went overboard with the invitations and invited a lot of 'high-profile persons' that I happen to know as well," she explained, giving a playful wink.

"But do not let them scare you all. You will fit right in. These people couldn't care less about your background or the work you do. They are just here to have a fun time. Besides, everyone knows I only invite people around me that are worth being in my inner circle. So, let your hair down and relax!" She waved over a waiter to pour them some champagne. "You don't have to tell me twice," Tiffany said as she pushed her boobs up, showing more cleavage. Everyone laughed. Several hours later, everyone found their little chill spot. Tiffany knew there was a pool, so she changed into her sexy swimsuit. She posed seductively in the pool drinking her wine, while conversing with a handsome guy who seemed interested in her. Tessa and her boyfriend Todd, found a long-lost friend that they knew in high school, so they wasted no time catching up. Sonya and Marge found a table with people of their age group playing a card game they loved, so they decided to participate. Sequoia smiled to herself as she watched her friends have an enjoyable time.

"I take it from that smile you are having yourself a good time," a husky male voice spoke from behind her. She turned to see a tall handsome guy in a red shirt and black jeans. He looked ordinary but at the same time, his presence was captivating. His shoulders and chest were broad, and he stood towering over her just a little. His eyes were blue like the sea and his lips were red as strawberries. He was incredibly attractive, and Sequoia could feel herself drawn towards him. It was obvious the females who were nearby were also captivated by his looks and a hint of jealousy lingered in their eyes.

"I am Sean by the way," he said, stretching his broad hands to meet her tiny palms. She was so hypnotized by his looks, she never even realized she was shaking his hand for a long while. When she did, she blushed and quickly pulled away. He laughed. "I am... um… Sequoia."

"Nice to meet you. You look exceptionally beautiful this afternoon." "Th... Thanks." "Do you want to go somewhere quieter to talk?" "Where do you have in mind?" "The balcony is less crowded, and I think there is an empty table there." It was as if her feet were moving but her mind was at a standstill as she did not even remember holding his hands. The next thing she knew, they were on the balcony seated on bar stools with a table between them.

"What would you like to drink?" He asked. "I would like a long island iced tea." "Wow. Can you manage that?" He said giving her a sensual look. "Off...course." He waved over a waiter who brought their drinks in no time. There was something about him that made her desire to stay in his presence forever, but she had to snap herself out of that dream. She knew that a guy like him was only interested in one thing, which was sex. She then finally came back to her senses after several minutes of conversation.

"So, what kind of work do you do?" he asked. "Well, I work as a..." Many thoughts crossed her mind as she took a long sip of her drunk. Heck, she was never going to see him again so she might as well lie. "I work as a financial adviser." "Wow, that is great. Do you mind if I ask where?" "Yes, I mind," she replied, smiling. "Okay, sorry if I was prying too much."

His phone then rang and after a brief conversation on his phone, he said, "It was great meeting you. I wish I could stay and talk more but I have a little emergency. Can I get your number so we can arrange to meet again?" "Sean, you're a nice guy and it was really great meeting you as well, but I am going to pass on that." He looked a bit shocked at first, but then he composed himself before he wore his shades and stepped away from the table.

"Well, I respect a lady's wishes. I hope we do meet again someday... Sequoia." And with that, he walked away leaving his fresh scent of morning breeze surrounding the table. Her heart cringed, wondering if she had made the right decision. There was just something about how he mentioned her name. Quickly, she dismissed the thoughts occupying her mind and made her way back through the crowd to find her friends.

CHAPTER FOUR

It had been two weeks since Lisa's party, but as the gang sat in the cafeteria at their usual table, they realized Tiffany had been absent from work for a couple of days. "We know where she lives, and she has always welcomed us into her home," Tessa said. "She is neither answering our texts nor calls. We owe it to her to just make sure she is okay," Sonya added. Marge and Sonya nodded in agreement. "Well, it's settled. Tessa will drive us to Tiff's place so we can check on her," Sequoia concluded.

They knocked on the door a few times before Tiffany finally decided to answer. When she opened the door to let them in, Sequoia noticed she was unkempt. Her hair was messy, and it looked like it had not been combed for days. Her mascara looked old and stained and her eyes were baggy. Inside the house was untidy; there were dirty dishes in the sink, broken glass on the floor and clothes lying everywhere. Immediately, they knew something was wrong, as this was not Tiffany. They all sat down on the wide couch across the small coffee table from Tiffany, who looked nervous. "Tif, what is going on? We are sorry to drop in like this, but you were not answering our calls and messages..." Marge started.

"And you haven't been to work for five days now," Tessa interjected. Everyone looked concerned as they sat silently, waiting for a reply. The silence went on for a few more minutes before she spoke. "Sam raped me." Jaws fell wide open, and everyone stared first at each other, then at Tiffany wondering if they heard clearly. "What do you mean by..." Sequoia began to ask but Tiff interrupted her.

"I said Sam raped me! He raped me! Damn bastard raped me!" Her voice grew louder as tears poured down her cheeks. Immediately, everyone huddled around her, but she prevented anyone from touching her. She held her hand up and spoke. "Remember that night after work when I asked you all to go ahead without me? It was because Sam said he wanted to take me out that night. I changed at work, and he said I should meet him in his office so we could walk down together. When I went to his office, he started touching me all over! Initially, I thought he was just messing around but then it became serious. I told him to stop, but he would not. Next thing I knew, he lifted up my dress and bent me over on his table. Then he put a gun to my head and he... he ra...raped me!"

Her voice broke as tears rolled down her cheeks. Everyone empathized with her and started crying as well. "I did not go to the police. He threatened me and besides, who would believe a low-life housekeeper to a well-known businessman who has powerful connections."

The group gave her the time and space to vent. They neither judged her nor bombarded her with questions. They just empathized with her and offered their best advice the entire evening. After they calmed Tiffany down, Sonya and Marge made her dinner while Tessa and Sequoia cleaned up the house. Before they left, they each gave her a warm hug that put Tiffany a bit more at ease. Several thoughts crossed Sequoia's mind after she got home. She was angry at Sam for what he had done to her friend. She knew what it felt like to have your body violated by someone you thought you could trust. It was not going to be easy for Tiffany to heal from that ordeal and so, once everyone was busy in another room, she used the opportunity to talk to Tiffany and give her a card for a good psychologist that could help her through this tragedy.

Tiffany took a three-week leave from work, after which she returned. She was never the same bubbly and talkative Tiffany again; she had changed. She had become quieter and often spaced out between conversations. Tiffany's shift was nearly over when she asked Sequoia to assist her in cleaning the bathrooms that were on the floor where Sam worked. They were almost finished cleaning the male bathroom. Sequoia went into the last stall to clean the toilet, while Tiffany cleaned the sinks. Just then, the bathroom door opened, and Sam walked in.

"Look what we have here!" he bellowed. Sequoia stopped what she was doing and listened attentively.

Tiffany ignored him and continued cleaning. "Hey, bitch, I am talking to you!" He shouted, grabbing her hand, and causing her to grunt in pain. "Do not touch me you monster! Take your damn hands off me!" "Or what, huh? What are you going to do about it?" "It's not what she is going to do, it's what I am going to do." Sequoia emerged from the stall silently so that he did not notice her. She had held the mop tightly in her hands in a battle stance. She had a stern and bold look on her face.

He released his grip and looked at Sequoia with animosity, who also returned the stare. "I know what you did, you psychopath." "You cannot prove anything, you crazy bitches. You better keep your mouths shut before I make both your lives a living hell." "Oh, really now? Is that so? Why don't you come closer and put your words into action?" Sequoia walked up closer towards him with a deadly stare in her eyes.

"Sequoia don't!" Tiffany begged. "I am not afraid of scums like you, Sam, so if you think your little words and money can scare me, then you are wrong. You know nothing about me so back the hell off." Sequoia squeezed the mop tighter as they stared into each other's face, while keeping her stance. He was just about to make a comment when the bathroom door rattled and in came a staff member. At this point, they both had relaxed, and Sam exited the bathroom, slamming the door behind him. The girls quickly finished and went to their locker room.

"I saw a different Sequoia today. Like girl! Who are you?!" Tiffany asked. Sequoia shrugged and smiled as she began to remember her past. After what happened to her with her stepfather, her mother made sure she could defend herself. Her mother had her take self-defense classes with her. "It was just an impulse. I hated how he was treating you," she answered. "Thanks for the backup but remind me not to ever get on your 'impulsive' side ever," Tiffany joked. The others soon joined them, after which they all went down the elevator together and dispersed to their separate ways home, except

Sonya and Sequoia who stayed back. They walked to a nearby park after the others left. At the park, Sequoia told Sonya what had happened with Sam. So, Sonya proposed a plan with Sequoia regarding Sam, to which she agreed. All Sequoia had to do was find out the places Sam frequently visited and relay the information back to Sonya. "Remember to keep this between you and I. Nobody else needs to get involved, especially Tiffany." Sequoia nodded. "We will discuss any latest information you gather at our spot. Once it is done, we will never speak about it... ever. Not to anyone... you hear me child? Clean, short, and simple." "Definitely, you have my word," Sequoia said. A memory flashed in her mind when she had a conversation like that with her mother.

The next few days, Sequoia kept a close eye on Sam while he was at work. Any garbage he disposed of, either in his office or anywhere on the work premises, she searched for any receipt that could be useful. Finally, after two weeks of snooping, she noticed a pattern on his receipts. Every Thursday evening, he went to a specific sports bar for a drink. She relayed that information to Sonya so she could get the plan in motion.

A few days later, news spread at the office that Sam was beaten into a coma by a group of five masked men, outside Barny's pub. Several of the staff were saddened by this but not Sequoia and the others. They knew he deserved this for what he had done to Tiffany. *Did you hear what happened to Sam*? Sequoia sent a text to Tiffany because she was home on her day off.

No, what happened? Tiffany replied. Sequoia typed a message telling her of what she heard had happened. Tiffany replied with a surprised emoji and followed it with: *Wow, Karma is a bitch! Wish I was there to throw a punch too*. Sequoia laughed to herself upon reading Tiff's reply. A week later after the incident, Tiffany invited the group to a restaurant for a little get-together dinner. Everyone showed up, not knowing what to expect. Tiffany RSVPed a nice cozy booth at a secluded spot for the five of them.

Once they were seated around the table, they ordered their meals and not long after, they were dining and talking. But nearing the end of the meal, Tiffany interrupted their conversations. "So, I know you are all curious about what this special occasion is about. But first, thank you all for being here." "Thank you for paying for this meal," Sonya added, and everyone laughed. "You're welcome. You all deserve it." She sighed deeply before continuing, "Meeting you all was the best thing that had ever happened to me. I never really had a family that loved me, except my sister. But you all made me feel like I belonged, after my own family disowned me for not living by their 'rules'. I know I have told you all the story already, but it was one of the lowest points in my life and that is how I ended up here. I ran off with a guy that promised me the world, though my family hated him; I was head over heels in love with him. Then a few weeks after I came here, we broke up and he stole everything from me. Luckily, I had a little money saved up which was hidden and that was how I was able to get by. When I got the job as a housekeeper, I hated it. I knew if my family found out what I was doing they would call me a disgrace. Honestly, I did feel like that initially but after I met you lovely people, I did not feel alone. I did not feel obligated to try and fit into society to be seen or heard. You all made me who I am, and I just want to say, I love you all."

"We love you too, baby girl!" Sonya said. Everyone nodded in agreement. "But..." She swallowed hard and sadly looked at everyone. Everyone paused to listen. "But I cannot tell you I am the same person I was a month ago after... after what Sam did." Her eyes became teary as she continued, "I have tried so hard to be strong, and yes, I thank you all for your support and love, but nothing can ever erase that night from my mind. I have been seeing a psychologist which has helped tremendously but I think for me to truly heal, I must leave these bad memories behind."

"Wait, what?" Tessa asked. "What do you mean?" Marge said as she placed her wine glass down. "I have been considering it since the day it happened, but you have all been so supportive, so I did not want to just leave abruptly. But now, I feel more confident that I can do this... I know he is not at work anymore but just being at work and passing by his office is like a constant reminder of what happened. It had taken a huge toll on me. I know I may look well on the outside and it may look like I am coping but deep down, I am drowning guys." She started to break down in tears. "I cry myself to sleep every night and I wake up terrified because of all the nightmares I have been having of him. I bite my nails so hard until my fingers bleed; something I had stopped doing years ago. I just feel like I am suffocating inside and the only way I can heal is to let go of this place and its bad memories."

"We understand," Sequoia managed to say but everyone was just staring at her with sad and tearful eyes. "I reached out to my sister in Arizona, and she was so thrilled to hear from me. I told her what had happened, and she wants me to come live with her. So, I am leaving tomorrow at noon; my flight has been booked." Everyone gasped in surprise. "That is a bit short notice," Tessa said gloomily. "I know. I knew if I told you all earlier, you would try to talk me out of it and make me feel even worse than how I am feeling now about leaving. But I need this. Please understand. Please, forgive me." "Well, I know what you went through was life changing and I cannot imagine what you have been going through these past weeks. But though it saddens me... saddens us all, we understand. But we are sure going to miss you," Marge finally spoke.

"Yes, we will never forget you, hun," Sonya added. "You have been a great friend," Tessa said. "Thanks for always brightening up our days. You made coming to work worthwhile," Sequoia said. "Thank you, guys. I really appreciate it. I will miss you and I will never forget you all. I still have that picture we took together at that fair a year ago. I will keep it close to my heart and whenever I feel down, I will look at it to remember the reason I have hope." They did a group hug and took a group photo.

"So, I am just traveling light — only my clothes and other personal stuff. I am leaving my spare key with you all so you can take my furniture and anything else you want. I just paid rent, so you all have enough time to move the stuff out before the landlord reclaims the room," Tiffany said. They spent the next few hours reminiscing on the good times they had together. It was a night of friendship, laughs and sadness.

CHAPTER FIVE

Two weeks had passed since Tiffany left, but the group was still adjusting to life without her. It was the end of the shift, so Tessa and Sequoia made their way to the lobby area. They were seated in a corner waiting for Marge and Sonya to join them when Sequoia heard a familiar voice. When she looked behind her, she was shocked to see who it was….it was Sean! The guy she met two months ago at Lisa's party. He was surrounded by five bodyguards and a lady, dressed in full blue that looked like his assistant. She quickly looked away from them and blurted out softly.

"Tessa, that's the guy I told you about that I met at Lisa's party." She was almost in shock as her hands gripped the chair handles. "What the... OMG! I cannot believe it! You blew off Sean Ebanks???!! The well-known billionaire who happens to own the tech company called 'Stack Up'!!!!!" "Shhhh, keep your voice down!" She glanced in their direction, but they were busy talking to a small crowd that surrounded them. Then, she spotted Ashley in the midst.

"Sorry, but if I knew it was that Sean, I would have slapped you into next week." "I did not know he was a billionaire okay! And OMG, I did not know he owned Stack Up!" "Yeah, and a bunch of other popular companies! Girl, I am ashamed to call you my friend." "Look, I did not know okay! And besides, he is not my type!" "Waiiit.. not your type? He is every girl's dream. He is rich, cute, and sexy. You are crazy." "I am not talking about his physical looks; I mean personality wise."

"Who cares about personality when you are getting all that dough. "Sequoia shook her head in amazement. "Look, I just do not think we would be a good match. Besides, a rich guy like him probably has many women swimming in his pocket... literally. I do not want to be a part of that census." "Anything you say sister. Gosh, if I were single I would..." Sequoia pinched her on her side and Tessa jerked a little. "Ouch! All I am saying is, he is hot!" They both laughed.

The next day, as soon as Sequoia walked into the locker room, Tessa pulled her aside to talk with her. "I heard that Mr. Ebanks is doing some sort of collaboration and investment in the company. He will be here for two weeks, having various kinds of meetings for some upcoming business deal!" she said with excitement in her voice. Sequoia's heart began to race as she fell in a seat nearby. "No, No. You are joking right?"

"Nope, Lisa gave me the scoops. Why the long face?" "I told him I worked as a financial adviser. Now, when he sees me as a housekeeper what will I say, 'Hey, I lied to you to look smart.'" "Oh wow! I did not know you told him that. Well, he might not remember you. I mean it has been two months, right?" "But what if he does remember me?" "Well, then you're screwed." She shot her a stern look.

"Okay! Okay! Just avoid him for the next two weeks. The meetings are normally held in the boardroom on the sixth floor, on the other side of the building. There is no way your paths would cross."

"You're right! And we are assigned to clean the third and fourth floor. We never get the opportunity to go up to that side. You are a genius." "I know. But Sequoia... you said it yourself; he is not your type. So why are you all worked up about it if he sees you like this? I mean, why would you care?"

She started thinking to herself... *why should she care? I mean, he does not mean anything to me. I do not even know the guy*. But deep down in her heart, she knew she felt something more. She shrugged, "I know, but I lied to the guy about being a financial adviser. So, what if he sees me, finds out I lied about my work and tells Ashley? She would make my life a living hell than it already is." That was not the real reason, but she nailed it. "Yeah, that's true."

The rest of the day went by quickly, and Sequoia was relieved that she went through the day without running into Sean. For the next few days, Sequoia focused on staying hidden, especially the day Ashley took Sean on a tour of the building. It was a close call when Tessa sent her a text, telling her that they were headed to her side of the building. So, she had to hide in the janitor's closet for almost thirty minutes.

It was obvious a lot of the female workers were fascinated with Sean. Sometimes, while cleaning the offices, Sequoia could hear them gossiping about him. One rumor that went round was Ashley was one of the females who kept flirting with him. Sequoia's blood boiled, especially when Tessa told her she heard that they went on a lunch date. She thought to herself... *why was she mad? She barely even knew the guy. Why did she feel so jealous*?

The two weeks were nearly over, and things were going as planned. Sequoia had just finished her shift and changed off into her casual clothes. She stood by the elevator waiting for Tessa, Marge, and Sonya, when she heard the elevator ding. When she looked up from her phone, standing in front of her was Sean Ebanks. Her heart started to race but she kept her cool, telling herself that he may not remember her; she planned to do the same. "Sorry, I will take the next elevator," she said pressing the button but to her surprise, a twisted smile spread across his lips. He stopped the elevator and stepped out with his entourage behind him, including the female friend she saw with him the other day.

"Wow! We meet again, Sequoia." She felt her legs almost give way; she had to lean against the corridor's railing. The look he gave her was breathtaking. "Umm…Hi…um…." She stumbled to find the right words. She felt so dumb around him. "Do not tell me you have forgotten such a handsome face already. It is Sean, from the party some time ago." She forced a smile and said, "Yes, I know... I mean yes... Sean. I am Sequoia... but you just said that." She bit her lip as her cheeks flushed red. "It's okay, girls always get a bit tongue-tied around me... so, this is where you work?"

She hesitated. "Ahh, still secretive, aren't we? It is okay, I respect that. Were you headed down? Can we ride together?" "Actually, I was waiting on my friends. Sorry, I…" "It's okay, Sequoia, go ahead." The moment she turned, she saw Tessa, Marge and Sonya smiling. "Yeah, we will be fine darling. Do not refuse this nice gentleman," Sonya said. "Shall we?" Sean asked. He waved to them as he ushered a speechless Sequoia into the elevator. "So, these are my bodyguards so do not be afraid. They will not bite. That is unless... you try to bite me."

He winked at her as he spoke. "And this is my assistant and good friend, Amber." Amber gave her a quick emotionless smile before returning to her phone screen. "Don't mind her, as she is always busy." "That's what you pay me for." He chuckled. Once they reached the lobby, Sequoia could feel all eyes on her. She knew she was the most envied right now, so she tried to avert everyone's gaze. "Give me your phone."

To prevent creating a scene, she handed him her phone without hesitation. He tapped the screen a couple times before handing it back to her. Then he leaned in and whispered in her ear, "That is my number. I want to take you to dinner tomorrow night. If you are interested, text me. If not, then I will know your answer." He then left with his entourage towards two Audi cars that were parked outside. His voice and smell left a yearning sensation on her skin. She could still feel his warm breath on her ear. Shortly after, Tessa and the others joined her, laughing their hearts out.

She shook her head at them and scolded them. The next day was her day off. She held her phone in her hands for hours, staring at his number and pondering whether she should accept his invitation. Eventually, she started typing him a message. *Hey, it is Sequoia. I would love to go out tonigh*t. She stared at the message for a couple of minutes then she deleted it and typed another text. *See you tonight? - Sequoia.*

She hit send and five seconds later, he responded. *Great, pick you up at 7. Send me your address.* She knew she could not let him know where she lived, so she quickly messaged Tessa asking her if she could get ready at her house. She agreed and so she gave him Tessa's address. She was shocked when he picked her up in a Bugatti Chiron 2024. "I know you're rich and all, but this is too extravagant for me," she told him. "Wow, I never had a girl tell me that, let alone tell me their honest opinion." "Well, there is a first time for everything." "Yeah, I like that." She looked at him, puzzled.

"Like what?" "I like a woman who can tell me their honest opinions. You are upfront and I like that." She raised her eyebrow as she tried to hide her flattery. Minutes later, they arrived at an exquisite restaurant. They picked a table in a secluded but beautiful spot that made her feel comfortable. They talked for hours, and Sequoia felt herself opening up to him. This was not what she expected as he was humble and thoughtful. He respected her boundaries and never forced her to talk about her personal life. He was not condescending like most rich men she had met before. Was he just pretending or was he for real? Unfortunately, she could not tell.

At the end of the night, he told her that he invested in their company, and he was going to spend a couple of months at their office building. He also added that he had several other business meetings around the vicinity, so he would be visiting Zenith Capital Industries on a scheduled basis. He already had an office set up on the fifth floor. This made her feel a bit more relaxed, knowing she had information about his scheduled meetings. Now, she knew which exact days he would be at the office so she could avoid him.

CHAPTER SIX

Weeks flew by quickly, and Sequoia found herself going out on more dates with Sean. She got to know him more, but she kept most of her private life a secret. What she liked about him most of all was he agreed and respected her decision in keeping their relationship from the public and her workplace. On weekends, he took her to different car race shows, where he showed her his race car and introduced her to the driver. He took her horseback riding, bird hunting, to the movies, charity shows, auctions and elite parties. She had never had so much fun in her entire life until now. For two months, she was able to keep Sean in the dark that she was a housekeeper though she was spending a lot of time with him. It was like she was living a double life.

Sequoia had just finished mopping the floor when she was paged to clean a spill by a water cooler in one of their board rooms where a meeting was taking place. She felt confident going to the boardroom, knowing that Sean was in Dubai. The room was dimly lit with just the projector screen giving off some light. Ashley was busy giving a presentation but from the corner of her eyes, Sequoia knew Ashley was watching her. Sequoia finished mopping and was just about to leave when Ashley asked her for a glass of water. She muttered as she walked towards her with the glass of water. ".... And now, let us invite Mr. Sean Ebanks to the podium, who will talk more about our collaboration."

At the sound of his name, she dropped the glass and it shattered. She panicked and stooped to pick up the shattered pieces of glass with her bare hands and she cut her finger deeply in the process. "Oh, for Christ's sake child! I gave you one simple task, and you made a big mess of it. Can you get any clumsier? Sometimes, I wonder about your mental health." Ashley rolled her eyes as she scoffed and looked down at her.

But Sean rushed to her side and helped her up. "Mr. Ebanks leave her be, as she can head to the med bay herself. That girl is always seeking attention to herself wherever she goes." Sean ignored Ashley's comments and tied his white handkerchief around her bleeding finger. Before he could say anything to Sequoia, she quickly disappeared from the room. She met Tessa outside the door. "Hey, what happened? I got a page to clean up some spillage. I thought you were..." Then she looked down at Sequoia holding a bloodied cloth then up at her distraught face.

"OMG! Girl are you okay?" Suddenly, Ashley peered her head from the door and interrupted, "Are you housekeeping? Enough chit-chat and come clean this place. I have an important meeting here." Tessa gave Sequoia a sympathetic smile before she left. Sequoia had a minor panic attack in the bathroom, so her friends gave her time to recuperate while they covered the rest of her shift for her. Her shift was almost done, so she sat in the break room replaying what had happened a few hours ago in her head. Her finger also throbbed with pain as she bit back the tears. A soft knock at the door startled her, so she quickly regained her composure. The door opened and in walked Tessa.

"Hey, hun, you have a visitor," Tessa said, scooting to the side and Sean walked in. Sequoia looked back at Tessa who mouthed the word 'sorry' before closing the door behind him.

"Can I sit?" She nodded and he sat across from her. "How is your finger? You look like you are in pain." "I am fine," she said, avoiding eye contact. "Let me see it." She shrugged and hesitantly gave him her hand. He gently pulled the bloodied cloth away and she winced in pain. "Sorry. Looks like it was a deep cut. Did you go to the med bay? This need sutures." "The nurse had already gone home by the time I passed by."

"Well, let me take you to the hospital and get you sorted out." "No, I am fine. I do not like hospitals." The real reason was she had no insurance, and she did not want to be embarrassed, especially given that she already had an outstanding medical bill there.

"Okay, I have a private doctor friend. We can go to his office. Do not worry about expenses." "I don't need your pity or your help Sean, I will go to the clinic tomorrow." "Tomorrow?! Baby, I know you're in pain and there is no way you can sleep through that pain tonight."

She knew he was right. "And besides, that is a high risk for infection there... Please, Sequoia, let me help you. Please." She looked into his pleading eyes and found herself agreeing. "The boundary for our relationship remains. I will meet you at your car in the underground parking lot." "Sure, anything for you." The doctor's visit was not bad. The painkillers really helped, and she felt a little bit better.

She sat in his car outside her "supposed" driveway to her house. She had been having him drop her at this house for the past few months. Interestingly, it was just five houses down from where she lived but he did not know that. Luckily, the person who owned that house was on vacation in another country for a couple of months.

"You have not asked me about the incident that happened in the boardroom. I mean what you saw..." "What I saw was a very hard working beautiful young lady, who was doing her job."

She looked at him with dilated eyes. "Sequoia, I know you are a very secretive person and I know you have your reasons why you are like that. I will never judge you based on your background, work, or ethnicity. I will still respect you and I want you to know that you can trust me enough to tell me your personal stuff. I know it will take some time for me to gain that trust, but I want you to know that beneath this suit and all this money, I am a human being, too."

He kissed her gently on her cheeks. "Have a good night, my sunshine." She was speechless. All she could do was smile at him while she exited the car and watched him drive off. For the next five months their relationship flourished. They spent more time together after work. Sean even invited her to meet his parents at a party they were hosting in Singapore. Sequoia was nervous as hell after their flight landed. They checked into a beautiful hotel where they had a fleeting time getting ready for the party.

It was a huge mansion with hundreds of people dressed elegantly. Sequoia fitted in so well; she wore a blue satin dress that accentuated her curves perfectly. Her long brown hair fell evenly at her waist, with a nice blue flower tucked at the side. Sean wore a black suit with a blue tie; he looked ravishing. He introduced her to his parents who loved Sequoia's beauty and her charming personality. He met her sister Claire, who was also welcoming towards her. Everything was going great until a tall, slim, red head approached the group. It was obvious his parents knew her.

"Hi Sean, long time no see." She gave him a flirtatious smile as she pushed between him and Sequoia to hug him. She pretended as if Sequoia did not exist. Sean returned her smile with a fake smile.

"Hello Sophia... this is Sequoia, my girlfriend." He walked around her so he could be at her side. Sequoia stretched her hand to greet her, but Sophia ignored her gesture. Instead, she deflected by sparking a conversation between Mr. & Mrs. Ebanks. After Sophia ended her conversation with the Ebanks, she turned back to Sean. "Sorry about that... Sequoia, right?" Sequoia nodded. "I do not know if Sean gave you a proper introduction, but I am Sophia Champagnie, C.E.O of Star luck's cafe and Sean's ex-wife." She choked on her champagne as she stared at them in shock. "Oh, he didn't tell you he was married once?"

"Sequoia, it was a long time ago. Our parents pushed us to get married right after we completed high school." "Pushed? Is that what you are calling it now? We were happily married for what? Three years before you decided to cheat." "I am not doing this now with you Sophia. You always try to push the people I care about away. You need to move on. And if you cannot get your ass out of your head and be civil, then we will go elsewhere." Sophia's vindictive smile turned into a frown. There was an awkward silence that lingered in the air for a couple of seconds between the trio. The Ebanks were still engaged in their own conversations, unaware of what had just transpired. Sophia cleared her throat asking, "So, Mr. and Mrs. Ebanks, are you guys still planning on going to that retreat?"

While they spoke, Sequoia sipped her champagne slowly as she looked around the room. She was just about to ask to be excused when Sophia roped her into the conversation.

"So, Sequoia, how did you and Sean meet? I missed that part. Was it at one of his business meetings? What kind of work do you do?" It was obvious Sophia was determined to get a comeback after that little intense moment she had with Sean. Her questions sparked Mr. & Mrs. Ebanks attention which was no doubt the intended aim. Sequoia looked nervously at Sean who was about to comment when Sequoia blurted out.

"I am a housekeeper at one of his business investment groups, but we met before that at a mutual friend's party." Everyone stared at them for a while before breaking out into laughter. "Wow, she is funny, too," Sophia said. Mr. and Mrs. Ebanks joined in the laughter, but Sean and Sequoia wore a straight face. "It wasn't a joke," Sean said. "Wait... what?" Mrs. Ebanks retorted. "You're serious? She is a housekeeper?" Mr. Ebanks added. "This is the funniest thing I have heard all night," Sophia said sarcastically.

"You brought a housekeeper to introduce as your girlfriend? Of all the women you have met, you brought a housekeeper here?" Mr. Ebanks asked. "You are an Ebanks for God's sake! You are a billionaire, and this is the best you could do?" "I am utterly disappointed," his mother joined in. "Can you all please shut up!" Sean said strongly.

"I am not sixteen years old anymore so you cannot tell me who to date or marry. I am a grown man who has made a successful life for himself. A life that you both take pride and joy in, boasting about to your rich friends. So, let us keep it that way. I do not need you all in my personal life. This is not a business investment. I love and respect Sequoia. She has been the best thing that has happened to me. Yes, I can have any woman I want, but I am tired of being with women who pretend to be someone they are not, just to be in my life. You married mom for love and vice versa so let me do the same. And I do not care if you both stop talking to me because of this. Do whatever you want because you have no hold over me, not financially and certainly not mentally. If you cannot accept her... then we are done here."

After that speech, he took Sequoia by her hand and walked away leaving his parents baffled and Sophia with a slack jawed expression. Several spectators who saw what happened looked in awe at the scene. Thoughts flooded Sequoia's mind as she heard Sean's words. He just admitted he 'loved her'. She was shocked at his words. Was she supposed to say it back? Did he mean it or was he saying it to make a statement?

CHAPTER SEVEN

Back at the hotel, Sean was enraged at his parents and Sophia's behavior. Sequoia had never seen him so angry before. He paced the room back and forth swearing to himself. Sequoia sat on the bed silently, caught up in her own thoughts of everything that had just transpired. She snapped herself back into reality and slowly approached a disgruntled Sean.

"Sean!" she said almost shouting, that made him stop in his tracks and turn to face her. She walked over to him and squeezed his hand. "Sean, it is okay, just breathe. They are not here now." "No, you do not understand. Those people I call my parents are always doing this..." "Doing what? Help me understand," she pleaded.

He sighed deeply as he ran his hand through his hair. "Growing up with them, they always tried to force their 'way' on Claire and I. It was like we had to be the best at everything, so I never really enjoyed my childhood or my college life. They were always in the shadows, pressuring me to do more and when I lashed out, they would threaten to cut me off financially. I had no choice growing up. I was forced into being this kind of guy."

He sucked in the air deeply and stared into her sympathetic eyes. It was obvious that he was emotionally traumatized by his parents growing up as she knew all about trauma. "Sean, it seems your past experiences growing up, took a toll on you mentally. But you cannot let it get to you. You are stronger now. They have no control over your life anymore." He chuckled briefly, "You sound like my psychologist." "Psychologist?" she asked, confused. "Yeah," he answered, waking to a table in the corner and pouring himself some whiskey.

"I started seeing one after I started working. I did not realize my parents had affected me so much until one day, I went through my girlfriend's phone or rather my ex I should say." He gulped down the liquor and poured himself another. "What happened?" "I had this girl at the time, Trisha. We had been together for eight months and I really liked her. I liked her because love does not come easy for a guy like me. I was still messing around with other chicks."

Sequoia felt a bit uneasy at hearing his comments, but she kept a straight face. He gulped down two more shots of whiskey. "Trisha was in the shower when a text came on her phone. I idly looked over at her phone screen that was laying on the pillow beside me. It was a message from her best friend, Gina saying, *Sean is a control freak...* the rest of the message was hidden so I unlocked her phone and decided to read the whole goddamn thing."

Sequoia watched him as he drank another shot, filled his glass, and sat at the edge of the bed. She later joined him on the bed. The scent of the whiskey was mixed with his breath. It was obvious he was getting a bit tipsy. "I became curious so I started reading their previous conversations and I found out Trisha was not happy with me. She saw me as a control freak that wanted to dictate her life. Those were her exact words. She felt trapped but she did not want to break up with me because I was freaking rich! So, that is when I realized I was turning into my parents, and I knew how it felt to be the victim. I decided to get the help I needed so I could be a better man but that was over ten years ago. I did not want to become my parents."

There was a thirty second pause after his explanation before he added, "I am sorry about not telling you about Sophia."

"My parents forced me to marry her as soon as we completed high school because her family were also billionaires. And yes, I did cheat on her with some college girls. But come on, I was young and dumb. I was not ready for commitment and my parents knew that but as usual, I had no say in it. They forced me to marry her against my will. They said if I did not marry her, they would not fund my college fees. Even that responsibility at such a young age scarred me. So yes, I am a messed-up guy with a messed-up past."

He was about to take another drink when Sequoia held on to the glass and pulled it away. "No more, Sean." He stared at her with sympathetic eyes and sighed. "Believe me when I say I know what trauma is and I know what it can do to you. But that is a story for next time... the point is, you are not alone Sean. You did the right thing when you decided to get the help you needed; many people would not have taken that step, especially for someone as wealthy as you. The fact that you saw your flaw and wanted to change, already makes you a better person. Nobody is perfect; your past may influence your future, but it does not have to control you. Yes, you are grateful for the opportunity your parents gave you but now you control your own life. They have no say in your choices because everything you accomplished was all on your own."

"Thank you, Sequoia. I really appreciated this. Other than my psychologist, you are the only person who knows this about my past." "You're welcome. I am here for you." They kissed passionately for a few minutes, until they cuddled in bed and fell asleep in each other's arms.

It was morning and the couple were packing the last of their belongings before they departed on their flight back home. "I apologize that you had to see that side of me last night, Sequoia. I had too much to drink and my parents just infuriated me. I should have not let it get..." "Sean, it is okay. You are only human. And besides, you cannot just show me your good side and expect me to fall in love. I need to see your ugly side too. I would rather see your bad side than live a lie with you."

He smiled and blushed as he stared at her. "God, you are so different from everyone else and that's what I love about you, Sequoia." She smiled as thoughts rushed through her mind. *There he said it again, love. Did he really mean it? Can a billionaire like Sean Ebanks who can have anything he wants in this world love someone like her?* Those thoughts continued to fill her mind all the way on the journey home.

A few weeks later, Tessa and Sequoia went into town to buy some coffee at Star luck's café —it was their day off. They sat down in a corner inside the café conversing when they happened to notice a tall, slim, red-headed lady emerge from a side door. She wore shades and had three bodyguards following closely behind her. She stopped midway in the café, conversing with the manager for a few minutes. It was not until the lady looked in their direction for a moment that Sequoia knew exactly who it was.

"Oh shit!" Sequoia distracted herself by taking a big gulp of her coffee. "What is it?" "Tessa, remember the ex I told you about that I met at the party?" "Yeah..." "That's her talking to the manager." "What the f...!" she exclaimed, almost choking on her coffee. "I remember the story, but yet again, you failed to mention she was one of the C.E.O's of the Star luck's café!"

"And again... I did not think that was important... but wait, how do you know that? Do you know her?" "Hello, you know I am a coffee freak, and my number one favorite coffee is Star luck. I know the names of the ancestors who built this place, and the current family who now owns the franchise which is the Champagnie family. And besides, who does not know Sophia Champagnie! I even follow her on Instagram."

"Well, apparently me…." "Do you think she saw you?" "I doubt she remembers me and besides even if she did, a hotshot like her is not going to come to talk with someone she hates." "Well... umm... I think you might have that wrong because she is walking over here." "Wait! What...the f---" Sequoia looked up to see Sophia strolling towards their table with a mischievous smile on her face. She removed her glasses, "You look so familiar, and I just had to take a closer look at you. I hope you do not mind," she said sarcastically.

"Cut the bullshit Sophia, you know exactly who I am," Sequoia said blatantly. Tessa's jaw dropped when she heard how her friend was speaking. "Excuse me? To whom do you think you are talking to? Do not address me on a first name basis as if we are friends. It is Ms. Champagnie to you, and might I remind you that you are in my café?" "Well, Ms. Champagnie, since it is your café, I am sure you should know your way around. My friend and I were not sitting in your path, so I do not see how you strayed all the way over here in the first place." She could see the burning rage in Sophia's eyes, but she knew all too well that her image and pride came first more than anything else, since several eyes were on them. So she maintained her composure, wore her shades and spoke a little loudly.

"Well, I apologize for the intrusion. I just thought you looked like someone I knew." She then lowered her voice to a whisper so that only Sequoia and Tessa could hear. "You know, men like Sean do not change easily my dear... a billionaire like that cannot be satisfied with someone as ordinary as you. Let us see how long it takes before he grows tired of his new toy?" With that, she strolled off with her bodyguards outside to a waiting tinted up BMW. Her words lingered in Sequoia's mind.

"Hey, do not let her get to you, hun. It is obvious she still has feelings for him. She is just trying to scare you." "Um... yeah, let's get back to what we were talking about earlier." Even though Sequoia brushed off the memory of what took place, she could not get Sophia's words out of her mind.

CHAPTER EIGHT

It was four o'clock in the afternoon when Sequoia heard someone pounding on the door that woke her up from her nap; she took a nap since she had a headache after she left the café. Before she fell asleep, she received a text from Sean telling her he was sixteen miles away, at a building called 'Zurtek' where he had a meeting. She knew that place; she always passed it on her way home. He had wanted to pick her up afterwards for dinner, but she declined; not because she was busy, but because of what Sophia had embedded in her mind earlier.

"I am coming, Stacey." Hesitantly, she went to the door to find an impatient Stacey.

"I am having a party and in the next thirty minutes, guests will be arriving. The party will have people from my workplace attending as well as my cousin that is visiting from Washington. They are all important high-profile persons and clients, so I need you to stay put and keep quiet here until seven o'clock." "What do you mean stay put?" "As in, no one needs to know you live down here so if you need to use the bathroom, do it now. Otherwise, use this bucket here and get rid of it in the night."

She held up a bucket in her hand as she spoke. Sequoia felt her blood boiling with rage at that level of disrespect. "...And I am going to need you to help me clean up afterwards so..." "Excuse me what?" Sequoia had a stern look on her face. "What? Do you not understand what I am asking of you? I said..." "No, I heard what you said but I am not doing that! I am not doing any of this! You are treating me like an animal!"

"Don't forget who you're talking to, Sasha!" "Or else what Stacey! No, this is not fair. I am a human being; I may not be able to help you financially but that does not mean you should treat me like crap. I have put up with a lot with you these two years and I have always done what you ask, but this time you are crossing the line." Stacey folded her arms in rage and said, "You have put up with a lot? Huh? What about me who has to put up with a grown ass stranger living in my garage for free. You do not pay bills; you do not do shit. It is not my fault you never finished school and made anything of your pathetic life than to be a lousy housekeeper. Even a prostitute makes more than you! Maybe that is what you should be doing instead of living off me and my two kids!"

Now, they were up in each other's face. There was tension in the room. "Do not go there! You know nothing about me and my life or what I have been through. At least I am not a hypocrite. You go around telling people you are a part of an organization where you help others who are less fortunate, but you make empty promises and then treat them like crap! We both know you only joined that organization because it builds your image, and you get monetary benefits every month. You say I love living off people, well, check yourself bitch because you are doing the same!"

Stacey was so shocked she could not reply for a few seconds but when she was about to, the doorbell rang. So, she threw the bucket angrily behind Sequoia.

"You will regret this!" she pointed at her before storming off. Sequoia slammed the door behind her and went back to bed. She was so angry and frustrated, but not long after, she fell asleep. This was one of her body's defense mechanisms in response to stress — sleeping it off for as long as she could.

An hour later, Sequoia could feel frigid air in the room and somehow, she knew the room was brighter. She rustled a bit under the covers before she decided to get up. When she sat up in bed and looked before her, she was flabbergasted at the several pairs of eyes staring back at her. Stacey stood with a vengeful look in her eyes, holding a glass of whiskey in one hand and pressing the garage remote button in the other.

"There she is! The girl who has been living in my freaking garage. She is a freaking ungrateful bitch who has nothing but disrespected me after I had done so much for her." She sounded drunk as she took a big gulp of the whiskey. "What's going on here?" A red-headed lady in shades emerged from the corner of the garage looking at Stacey. "Cuz, what are you doing?"

As she spoke, she looked towards the opened garage door and immediately she removed her shades, she saw Sequoia on the bed with flushed cheeks.

"OMG! My My look what we have here." A sly look and grin spread across her face. "She was the one I was telling you about Sophie…" Stacey said. "Give me the remote, Stacey," Sequoia demanded sternly. Sophia suddenly took her phone out and quickly snapped a picture. Sequoia was about to charge at them when Stacey threw the remote inside the garage but behind her. She quickly ran for it and lowered the garage door. The last thing she saw was the broad and evil grin on Sophia's face as she waved at her.

Sequoia felt queasy. Her body was still in shock and the only thing she could hear was her heart racing. She knew she was about to have a panic attack, so she quickly changed into her sweatpants and hoodie and dashed out from the house unseen. She wanted to cry but she could not as she walked obliviously. Her thoughts were all centered on what had just happened. Her life was ruined. Several hours later as she walked through the city, she felt raindrops on her head. Not long after, the rain started pouring heavily, so she scanned around the buildings for somewhere to take cover when she saw the Zurtek building across the street. She had been so caught up in her emotions that she never realized she walked all the way to the city and to where Sean was.

By the time she got inside she was soaked. A couple of people were in the lobby area staring at her, but she ignored them and went straight up to the receptionist. "How can I help you?" the receptionist asked, giving her an unfriendly stare. "I um... could you please tell Mr. Sean Ebanks I am here, and I need to see him now. Please?" "Who are you and is he expecting you?" "I am..." she paused as she thought of what to say. "I am Sequoia. He is expecting me." "Okay, let me check." The receptionist clicked a few times on the computer before she spoke. "I am sorry, but I do not see your name here." "Please, there must be..." "I said I cannot help you, miss... and if you would be kind to leave. You are wetting the floor," she said, eyeing Sequoia from head to toe and pointing out that she was dripping water.

Meanwhile, one of Sean's bodyguards that was standing nearby whispered into his earpiece. Then the bodyguard that was at the door of the meeting room nodded as he went inside the room. He silently went over to Sean who was seated with Amber, his P.A., at the meeting table. He whispered inaudibly in his ear and immediately Sean stood up in the meeting. "Amber, I have an emergency. Take over for me. I have to leave."

"But sir you're next to present. Are you sure..." "I said take over!" he said, giving her a stern look as she nodded at him. He quickly excused himself and made his way downstairs. When Sean got downstairs, he saw Sequoia walking towards the receptionist. "At least give him a call please, my phone got wet in the rain." As she spoke, she revealed her phone which was drenched in water. "Ma'am, this is the last time. I have had it with you. I am calling security."

"There will be no need for that." They both turned to see Sean walking towards them. Sequoia could not help but hug him tightly as she cried in his arms. He also hugged her back even though she was wet. "Sir, I... am sorry. I..." "Save your apologies, as I am not the one you should be apologizing to." He had never seen Sequoia so emotional. He knew that something was wrong, but he just consoled her.

"Tell them to bring the car around," he said to one of the bodyguards. Not long after, they were in his car driving to his place. He had given Sequoia some warm clothes to put on before they left. "Where are we going?" Sequoia finally spoke after minutes of silence. "My mansion. The one you have always declined my invitation to." She smiled briefly. "There it is, that smile. I thought I would never see."

As they approached his place, many thoughts crossed Sean's mind. He knew Sequoia was a secretive and mysterious person but something about those traits made him want her more. She was difficult to understand at times. He knew she was holding back because whenever he brought up any personal questions, she would immediately shut down or change the conversation. Normally, a guy like him would never have much interest in women who were difficult, but something about Sequoia made him want to stick around. With *her in this current mood would this finally be the moment she opened up about her past.* He thought to himself as the car came to a stop.

CHAPTER NINE

Once they reached his place, she showered and went downstairs for dinner. Sean had his personal chef make a traditional West Indian dish and this made Sequoia elated. The last time she tasted a well-done West Indian home cooked meal was when her mother was alive. Once they finished dinner, he took her to his cozy outside patio. They sat together on a big comfortable couch, with a beautiful fireplace in the center. Silence lingered in the air and then she spoke.

"I am sorry about bursting into your workplace like that. It's..." He hushed her. "Do not apologize for that. You mean a lot to me, and I am glad you came. That meeting was getting boring anyway." She giggled. "But what I want to know is what made my baby so sad… did someone hurt you?" She thought about everything that she had been through and how supportive Sean has been. She knew he at least deserved some of the truth. She took a deep breath in.

"I have panic attacks at times whenever I am stressed. This was brought on by a heated argument I had with the roommate I told you about and she said some hurtful things. The things she said brought back memories that I try to forget," she explained, shifting uncomfortably on the couch as she stared at the burning flames. "I know I have not talked much about my past experiences, and it is unfair as I know so much about you. At least, you deserve to know more, so here goes… I lived in Grenada with my mother who was a biochemist teacher. She met an American guy who had come to the island during one of his business trips and his name was Al Finster. They really liked each other and so they stayed in touch even when he went back to America. They became close and the next thing I knew, she told me they were getting married. It was a quick wedding and not long after we were migrating to America; I was sixteen years old at the time. After a year and a half, he started to treat my mom differently. They argued a lot and I think he hit her sometimes, but she tried to hide it. One evening, I came home early and only Al was home on the couch.

He seemed drunk so I sneaked to my room because I did not want him to know I was home. But I guess somehow, he knew I was home, and he came knocking on my door."

Her eyes became teary as she spoke. She could feel Sean's body tensing up beside her. "I did not answer. I just stayed quiet because somehow, I had a bad feeling in my gut. But he got upset and kicked the door in. Next thing I know he..." "Damn bastard!" Sean shouted angrily as he pulled her closer to his muscular chest. She sobbed hard as she tried to finish her story. "He raped me for two hours straight!" She cried louder as he hugged her tightly. Anger filled him as he listened to Sequoia crying. He gave her time until she was ready to talk.

"He threatened me afterwards and left to go to the bar. My mom returned home late, and she came straight to my room. She knew something was wrong as soon as she saw me. I could not control my emotions, so I broke down in tears and told her what happened. I could barely walk after that. My mom was so pissed, but she was silent. I kept asking her what she was going to do but all she did was start packing our clothes. After she loaded everything in the car, Al came home and saw us both sitting on the couch. My eyes were red and puffy, and I could not look at him. I remember him saying, "You little bitch you snitched." Then he ran from the room and returned with his gun. He said he would rather kill us than leave us to report him to the police and ruin his life. So, he shot at my mother but luckily, he missed, and the bullet only grazed her shoulder; she fell behind the couch, and she pretended to be severely wounded. I was so shocked; I never realized he was now standing right behind me with the gun held to my head. So, I closed my eyes waiting for my death when I suddenly heard him grunt in pain. My mom had snuck up on him and stabbed him. Once the gun fell from his hands, she used the opportunity to knock him unconscious. It all happened so fast. Then I remember my mom spat in his face before she dragged me to the car."

"Son of a bitch! Serves him right! He should be lucky she spared his life." Sequoia gave an uneasy smile. What she really wanted to say was that her mother stabbed him to death, thirty times and she stood watching the act. She never once stopped her mother while she had her revenge. If she told him this, would he think of her as a murderer? Would he look at her in a different light? Would he still want her if he learned she was an accomplice to murder? So many questions ran through her mind, but she had to maintain a straight face. She was not ready to trust him with that kind of information.

"My mom and I were wanted for the attempted murder of Al, and he was also determined to have his revenge. He even put up a reward for the capture of my mother and I, so we had to keep a low profile. Days after the incident, an opportunity presented itself and so we were able to leave unseen via the train station. We had to start a new life. My mom knew people who could help us stay off the grid and we did just that. One of my mom's connections was working on some documents to help us leave the state so we could live with one of her oldest friends where we would be safe. In the meantime, we were living in shelters, old buildings and sleeping at train stations. My mom taught me survival on the streets; I never knew my mom had this side to her. Shortly after we received our papers, we moved to another state. We went to live with my mom's friend, Kathy, and her daughter Serena who were nice people. Apparently, my mom knew Kathy from Grenada, but she left years ago before we came. My mom home schooled me, and she made sure I took self-defense lessons. She got a job as a waitress and helped Kathy out with the bills. It was like we were living a whole different life." "Sorry to interrupt, Mr. Ebanks, but can I get you or Ms. Lewis anything to drink?" The maid interrupted.

Sequoia and Sean declined the offer.

"Alright, I will be heading out now for the night." "Thanks, Mrs. Turner. Ed will be dropping you home tonight." "Thank you. God bless your soul," she said smiling and left. "Sorry about that darling, you were saying." "Um... oh yes, so everything was going well until my mom got sick. We found out it was pancreatic cancer, and it was progressing rapidly," she sniffed back the tears. "We could not afford insurance; hence we could not get the treatment she needed. Kathy did her best to help but it was too much of a financial constraint. I used to work three jobs just so I could have enough money for her chemotherapy and radiation treatment, but it was not enough."

Her tears began to pour down her already wet cheeks. "My mom told me to stop burning myself out and just let her die. It was so hard to let her go but I had to. That was the roughest year of my life… when she died." "How long ago was that?" "That was three years ago, and I was twenty-four years at the time… Anyway, a few months later, Kathy fell into bankruptcy and had to put the house up for sale. She had a sister in Colorado that was willing to let her, and Serena live with her, so I was on my own. After they left, I had to survive on my own. I rented a little one-bedroom rundown apartment to live in while I worked three jobs.

It was tiring and I did not get any time for myself. A good friend of mine who thought I deserved a fresh start invited me to some charity fair in the next town. I hesitantly accepted her invite. That is where I met my roommate, Stacey. Apparently, she was a part of a huge organization called C.A.R.E.S...."

"Yeah, I have heard a little about them. A lot of rich folks sponsor that organization. You were very lucky then." "Yeah... very lucky..." she said flatly, as she remembered what she had endured the last two years with Stacey. "So, Stacey was nice, and we got along well. I was tired of how my life was going so I started venting to her about how rough it had been. I did not tell her my personal life that involved Al or my mom. In the evening, when I was about to leave the charity fair because it was getting late, she called out to me. She said she thought about me a lot and wanted to help me out given that she had the means to do so. She said she would help me just until I got back on my feet, and I should not worry about repaying her back. In that moment, I accepted her offer and here we are."

At the back of her mind, Sequoia began to remember when she first moved to Stacey's house with her stuff; Stacey had her put them in the garage and she explained that it was only temporary. According to Stacey, even though it was a four-bedroom house, her two kids slept in two separate rooms and did not like people in their space. She said the fourth bedroom was run down and was still having 'renovations' being done to it. Conveniently, the renovations just happened to have lasted two whole years and were still ongoing. In addition to that, Stacey had her doing several chores in and around the house. It first started out as one chore that eventually turned into several chores and errands.

Whenever Sequoia would object, she would play the 'you're-not-helping-with-the-bills' card. Her thoughts were then interrupted by Sean, "I appreciate you sharing all this with me. I know it was not easy. Sequoia, you are a strong, diligent person. I wish you would not be so stubborn at times and let me help you out more, but you refuse… and I respect that. So instead, let me take you somewhere. I want you to forget about that roommate and all that wretched past and enjoy the present. I guess in some way like me, you never enjoyed life growing up. You were always fighting to survive, and you never had the chance to take a break and look after yourself. So let me do it for you. Let us take a week off so we can go to my cabin in California by the lakeside. You are going to love it."

"A week? Did you forget I am just a housekeeper? There is no way Mike is going to approve that many days off and at such short notice."

"Mike Peterson is your supervisor, right?" "Yes… what are you doing?" By now, Sean had started scrolling through his phone. He held up a finger at her and mouthed the words, "Just trust me." He spent a minute on the phone with Mike after which he hung up. "You have seven days off starting tomorrow. All he needs is a letter from you with the requested days. I just messaged Amber; she will take care of that." She stared at him in shock and speechless. "Wh---hat just happened?"

"Darling, I have a large share in that company, so they cannot say no to me. So, pack your bags. We are leaving tomorrow." "Wow, you never cease to amaze me…. About the packing part, I kind of do not want to go back to the house. I mean my roommate is..." "I understand, hun. We can stop at the mall and pick up some fresh outfits and a new cellphone for you before we head to the airport." He kissed her cheeks softly as she stared in shock at Sean who seemed really thrilled about the trip.

CHAPTER TEN

Before they boarded his jet, she sent a text to Tessa, Sonya, and Marge about her absence from work. They were excited and wanted to know every detail once she got back. She laughed to herself as she put her phone away. They arrived at a beautiful cozy cabin with a lake view. "No bodyguards or chef?" she joked. "Nope, it is about you and me this week. Besides, I have my safety measures in place; this place is impenetrable. Come on, let me show you around. You are going to love the panic room." She smiled and took his hand. Then he turned to her, "Oh, I will be your chef. I am not only a pretty face with a sexy body. I can help myself, too."

She laughed and squeezed his hand. He did in fact cook. They had grilled steak and fries out on his patio. It was a romantic sight to see, especially when she had the opportunity to witness a beautiful sunset. "...And so, I threw the cat into the fish tank." Sequoia laughed so hard she almost spilled her glass of champagne.

"OMG! Poor cat. Was he okay?" "Yeah, he climbed out himself. So, from that day, I learned that what you see in cartoons are not to be tried in real life." "You're crazy," she laughed. "Come on, I was four." After the laughter died down, Sean closed in the space between them and started kissing her passionately. She never knew her body was so hungry for his touch. He then lifted her inside and laid her gently near the fireplace still caressing her body. He removed his shirt and her dress. "Sean…."

He stopped and looked up at her. "I…I… Um since AI, I have never been…" He hushed her sweetly, "I figured. I promise I will be gentle as a rabbit…" She chuckled. "…but if at any point you want me to stop, I will."

She nodded and he continued kissing down her body until he reached her thighs. He gently removed her underwear and stroked her clitoris with his thumb.

He felt her body shiver at his touch. "It's okay, my darling..." he whispered. Then he lowered his soft warm lips and started kissing her labia. He kissed her a couple times before using his tongue to massage her insides. Her body curved in pleasure as she gripped his hair and moaned. His tongue was wet as he went deeper and deeper into her woman hood, with every inch of his tongue. Then he went back up to her breasts and sucked on her nipples. She then started begging him to enter her throbbing core. He ripped his clothes off and revealed his gorgeous manhood. They kept eye contact as he slowly entered her close-fitting woman hood. He felt her vaginal muscles tense up and then they relaxed as he went deeper. His thrust was slow at first and then he moved faster and faster. She felt like a million sparks were going through her body as pleasure engulfed her. They went on for hours until they were tired; they both climaxed and fell asleep in each other's arms. When she woke up, she was a bit sore, but it was worth it.

"Are you, okay?" he asked, looking over at her. "Yes, I am. It was great. Just a bit sore." "I can take care of that." He had a sheepish grin on his face. "How?" "A warm morning shower while I lick your wounds." She laughed as she saw the naughty look in his eyes. He lifted her up and in the shower they went. They spent the next couple of days hiking, fishing, and going on picnics. He even taught her how to drive. Then in the evenings, they would spend it making love for hours. They had just finished horseback riding in the valley and were now headed back towards the cabin. The horse trotted along an open grassy field, filled with flowers. The cabin could be seen in the distance.

"I am going to make you want me," he whispered in her ear. Instantly, she felt her body go numb as his hand rubbed her back gently. He then slowly moved his hand to the inside of her blouse, where he played with her bare nipples. They stiffened at his touch as she threw her head back onto his shoulders, moaning. He kissed her neck passionately as his hand gripped her breasts and massaged them in his palms. He let go of one of her breasts as he slowly moved his hand down her waist, past her skirt and then down her underwear. She was already wet when he fingered her vigorously, as the juice ran down his finger. He went deeper inside the heart of her femininity as she moaned. Her clitoris throbbed for more pleasure as her body moved with a sense of rhythm.

"You love that don't you." "Y…YES," she managed to say breathlessly. He pulled his hand out and licked his fingers, "Sweet." "Why did you stop?" "Open your eyes." She opened her eyes and realized they were now in the stables. "Wow… I…" He hushed her and lifted her down from the horse. They kissed passionately as he turned her backwards to lean over one of the empty stalls. He plunged his manhood so deep inside her that she cried out in pleasure. He spun her around to face him and then fixed his stiff shaft into her. He braced her back against the stall and thrust into her pool of moisture as he sucked her swinging tits. His tongue captured every essence of her body.

Her nails dug deep into the wooded pole against which she was leaning. His thrusts continued for several minutes until they both climaxed. He slowly withdrew his manhood and then he cradled her into his arms and walked back to the cabin.

CHAPTER ELEVEN

Once they returned to New York, she stayed at Sean's mansion, trying to avoid seeing Stacey. She did not even know if she was still welcome there. For all she knew, Stacey might have burnt her stuff or given them away to charity. She woke up to a chime on her cellphone; she had received an email. It was from a loan company that she visited a year ago, that had declined her application for a personal loan. She had wanted a small loan at the time to attend a local community college, get a few short courses done and then pursue a career in biochemistry like her mother. She read the email in disbelief as they had clearly now approved her loan and given her a six-month grace period before she started repaying the loan. This would give her plenty of time to budget and save. She felt relieved and happy, and all she had to do was sign the documents attached to the email and send a copy of the required documents to the loan officer. Also, they were giving her a bit more than she originally wanted, with a decent payback rate she could afford! It all seemed like a dream. She could even start looking for a small cheap apartment to live in for the time being.

"Thank you, God," she whispered to herself as she held the phone close to her chest. After basking in the moment, she looked up from her phone and saw a message from Sean. He had to leave early to go to an emergency meeting in Chicago and would return late in the evening. He assigned one of his chauffeurs, Tom, to take her to and from work. Then he added emojis at the end of his message: a tongue, water, and smiley face. She giggled at it, knowing what it meant. On her drive to work, Sequoia was glued to her phone scouting for apartments in her price range. She also did not want to waste any time, so she enrolled in a local college nearby. She was so caught up in her personal affairs, she never realized they had stopped.

"We are here Ms. Lewis," Tom said. "Oh, wow thanks. Have a wonderful day." "Thanks, and same to you." She got out of the car quickly in the underground parking lot, to avoid being seen and then she headed into the elevator nearby. Once she reached the building, Sequoia could not help but notice the several eyes staring at her. She felt uncomfortable and that was when the thought crossed her mind, *what if Sophia released that picture online of me in the garage??*

Her heart raced as she quickened her steps towards the elevator and averted the stares. When she entered the locker room it was empty, but she heard some muffled voices in the break room. She quickly changed into her uniform and rushed inside to see both Marge and Tessa seated around the table holding hands. When they looked up at Sequoia, she saw their eyes were red and puffy.

"Wh... what's going on?" Sequoia asked shakily. "My poor child. I did not want to tell you before you came to work." She looked at them confused as she walked slowly towards them. "It's Sonya... she... died last night," Marge said, as she broke down in tears.

Tessa hugged her as she wept. "Wha... what...???" Sequoia stood frozen for a couple seconds before she could comprehend what was going on. "She had a stroke last night and she died at the hospital," Tessa managed to say. Sequoia dropped to her knees and cried in anguish. Both Sonya and Marge were like mothers to her. Marge and Tessa both joined her on the floor and comforted her as they all wept. Now she knew why people were staring at her.

It was a long and sad day at work. Even their supervisor Mike looked sad, and they had a small gathering after work in remembrance of Sonya. When Tom came to pick up Sequoia, she asked him to stop by the park so she could take some time to herself alone to grieve; he respected her wishes. "I will be parked right here when you are ready ma'am," Tom said. "Thanks." She walked to one of her favorite spots where she and Sonya used to meet up after work. She leaned up by the railing and looked over at the ducks who were bathing in the small stream that flowed by.

She took a deep breath in as she remembered their last conversation and tears started to flow.

"I used to love coming here when I lived here." The voice sounded familiar, and Sequoia knew exactly who it was. She quickly wiped away her tears before turning to face her. "What do you want? Are you stalking me now?" She gave a sinister laugh. "Oh, please don't fool yourself. I am just taking my niece and nephew on an innocent stroll at a public park," Sophia answered as she gestured with her hand towards Amy and Josh, who were playing Frisbees nearby with a dog.

"I bought them a dog today. It is a very good animal to keep around so when strangers come into their house unannounced, it can drive them away," she said sarcastically. Sequoia rolled her eyes and hissed. "Just leave me alone, Sophia, please. Not today." "I just wanted to say hi. I mean, I have not seen you since that last time at my cousin's party. I have been staying at Stacey's place for a couple of days now hoping I would run into you." "For what reason?" "So, we could talk." Sequoia just shook her head dismissively. "We have nothing to talk about Sophia. I don't have time for this." Sequoia was about to walk away when she uttered, "Does Sean know you live in a garage? And does he know that you are an undocumented immigrant wanted for murder?" She stopped dead in her tracks and looked around briefly.

"Yeah, I figured that would get your attention, Sequoia or should I call you by your real name, Khushi Gupta?" "Shut the hell up before someone hears you!" Sequoia closed in on the space between them. "Be careful with your threats... you are in no position to be doing that." Sophia had a smirk on her face as she watched her intently. "So, my dear, will you please calm down? That temper is uncalled for." Sequoia's breath slowed down as she unclenched her fist.

"Are you finally ready to talk like a civilized person?" She nodded hesitantly. "Good." "I paid good money to hire a good friend of mine to dig up your past and I must say it took him weeks. He said your information was well hidden. He was going to give up when he found Serena." Sequoia eyes dilated with realization. "I see that name rings a bell. Anyways, he paid her good money and that was how she gave up your real name and from there, he was able to find the missing pieces. Let us see, where should I start." She circled Sequoia slowly like a vulture with a sly look on her face.

"You and your mom's green card expired and there was no way you could renew them because you were on the run after you both murdered her ex-husband in cold blood. But somehow, you both got someone good to forge fraudulent documents which claimed you were 'legal immigrants'.... must have cost you a fortune, given how long you have managed to fool everyone around you. Even poor Sean." "This is my life and my business... why are you making this your problem? Is this just about Sean? You broke up over ten years ago... he does not love you." Sophia laughed briefly and threw her head back. "Is that what he told you? Poor child. You should ask him what happened after we got divorced... you see, he may have told you that he never loved me, which was true when we were married but then he grew to love me. Yes, we got divorced and went our separate ways, but we ran back into each other a couple of years after. When he had just graduated from the university, we met up at a business party and old sparks really do not die because honey, he had his hands all over me in the lady's bathroom."

Sequoia scoffed as she shifted, uneasy on her feet. "Since that day, we have been hooking up. Every month, he flies to see me and sometimes I do the same... so forgive me if I was shocked when he showed up with you at his parents' party. It is party they keep every year, at the same time and place and where we always hooked up afterwards." Sequoia had a taut look on her face.

"Darling, I know all this must be overwhelming and in your small mind, you must be thinking I am lying just to get your attention, but as a businesswoman, I can assure you I always have my evidence." She then revealed her phone with a paused video on screen. "Look at it!" Sequoia turned her head away and frowned. "I swear to God, if you do not look at what I have to show you, Ms. Khushi, the immigration authorities will be here faster than you can say 'curry!'" So hesitantly, she looked down at the video. "Note the time and date at the top my dear."

She had an evil smirk as Sequoia gestured to the date which was a year ago. The video was two minutes long and showed Sophia and Sean having sex. Sequoia felt queasy so she turned away in disgust. Sophia stopped the video and placed the phone back into her pocket.

"So, you see my dear, that is why I said men like Sean do not change... I know the type of girls Sean likes and you are far from it. Sean does not want a filthy girl like you who has no class or stability. So have your fun now, but do not be surprised if he turns you into his personal maid for his house who he bangs on the side while he makes love to a 'Real' woman." For the first time Sequoia felt speechless as a million thoughts ran through her mind. "I know it is a lot to process in that bird brain of yours but know this... if you continue to have whatever it is you are having with Sean, I will leak all your documents to the immigration officers. Not only will you be deported back to your lousy little country, but you will be locked up in a tiny cell for years. And once the media gets hold of this, you can imagine the headlines, 'Top Billionaire Dates a Young Murderer.' His reputation would be tarnished, and he would lose all his wealth and businesses. His parents would hate your guts even more than they do now." She let out a sinister laugh.

"So, if I were you, I would stay away from Sean or I swear to God, you will regret this." Sequoia swallowed hard as Sophia gave her a mischievous wink before putting on her shades. "Bye, darling." She strolled off towards the children along with her bodyguards. Sequoia had mixed emotions as she went back to Tom to drive her back to the mansion. "Good news, Sean is back from Chicago, and he is waiting for you at the mansion, Ms. Lewis." "Good. Take me to him now!" She said angrily as she entered the car.

CHAPTER TWELVE

Soon after, she was at Sean's place. He was deep in conversation with his secretary Amber, when Sequoia stormed up to them. When he saw her, he attempted to give her a hug, but she just shrugged him off. "Hun, I heard what happened to Sonya... my condolences. I texted you several times after I landed but you did not respond." She ignored his comment and responded, "I want to talk to you... alone!" He could hear the rage in her voice. He looked at Amber who now looked worried as she stepped to the side.

"Okay... No disturbance," he said to Amber who shook her head. He then ushered her into his secluded study. "Do you want to sit?" "No, this won't take long." "Babe, what is wrong? Did some...?" "Be honest with me... have you been hooking up with Sophia after you guys broke up?" He had a shocked look on his face.

"I... where is this coming from?" "Answer the damn question, Sean Ebanks!" He sighed deeply and placed his hands in his pockets.

"Yes... we were having sex now and then but..." "But what, Sean? You failed to tell me about that part. You made it seem like after the divorce, you never once saw her again. You hid that information from me!" "I... just didn't think it was necessary because that is my past, which isn't who I am anymore!" "The past! You both hook up every year at your parents' party... how is that the past??" She walked across the room, groaning in frustration, "My God, there was even a sex tape with you guys a year ago!"

"Sex tape! Wait... she still has that?! We had an agreement for her to erase that years ago! She must have altered the date and time because that sex tape was several years ago!" "Oh, so you knew about the sex tape! OMG Sean, what else is there?!" "Wait... let me explain... Sequoia please, I haven't hooked up with her for almost a year now since I met you... I..." "Wow, so that is your excuse? So suddenly, she is the past.

We have been seeing each other for nine months now and I just started having sex with you last week. So, are you telling me you did not cheat on me with her or no one else???"

"Yes, that's what I am saying!" "I may be young, but I am not a fool. Men like you do not just change overnight. You are no different from your parents; you may not have been controlling me physically but emotionally, you were always in control. You played with me and my emotions! We are done, Sean... I do not want anything to do with you and you can burn my clothes because I want nothing to do with anything you gave me. Goodbye." "Wait, Sequoia, please don't...." She stormed out of the room with him following behind. "Tom, could you please drop me at Tessa's place?" Tom looked at Sean then at an upset Sequoia. Sean nodded to him, and he took her to the car. She saw the last look of sadness on his face when he stood on the steps and she drove away.

He marched furiously into his study and poured himself a couple glasses of whiskey. "Sean, remember your conference call in thirty minutes," Amber said as she stood by the doorway watching him attentively. "Reschedule it." "Wait... what?" "I said reschedule it. I do not want to make any calls right now." "But this is an important client... he..." "As far as I see it, they are the ones that want me to be a part of their company and not the other way around. So, if they really want this deal, they will not have a problem rescheduling it." He gulped down some more whiskey before throwing the glass angrily across the room, causing Amber to jump.

"I cannot believe that because of one simple girl, you are throwing away good business deals. Sean, why are you so hung up with her? I have seen you with so many women and you were never the type to be emotionally attached..." "I do not need your damn opinion, Amber! You may be a good friend, but you have no say in my personal life!" She was not afraid of him; no matter how angry he got as she knew him too well. "I am not interfering, but I just don't want you to mess up your career for someone like her... there are more..." He slammed his fisted hand on the table so hard that the bottle rolled off and broke.

"Someone like her! Don't you dare go there with me. Who are you to judge, huh? When I met you, you were a con artist going around and fooling old geezers for money, just to make a living. When people advised me to stay away from you because of your history, I never listened. I gave you the chance to be something greater. I gave you a job as my P.A. So, *someone like you* should not judge others. Keep your opinions to your damn self!" Amber had a remorseful look on her face as she spoke, "I apologize, I overstepped. If you excuse me, I will make that call and send the maid in here to clean up." Before he could respond, she exited the room quietly.

He then took his phone out and dialed a number. "Hello, you have not called this number in a long time. What may I do for you?" Sophia said coolly on the other end of the line. "Who gave you the right to tell Sequoia about what happened between us! Huh??" She laughed briefly and said, "Last time I checked, I was never sworn to secrecy. Besides, it was just an innocent little conversation." "I heard you were in town, but I thought you had left." He gave an empty laugh and continued. "You never change, do you? You always try to destroy my relationships in some way, but I want you to listen to me… if you ever talk to Sequoia again as much as come close to her or me, I am going to end you."

"End me? I want to see you try, Sean. Be careful of your threats… I still have a lot of secrets about you with evidence to back it up. I am sure Sequoia would love to see them." "Screw you, Sophia. I am not afraid of your threats. Do what you want to do but I am warning you, DON'T YOU EVER COME NEAR US AGAIN!!" With that, he hung up and threw his phone against the wall, breaking it into pieces. The maid had just walked in, and she jumped in fright. "Sorry," he said flatly before storming out the room. Once she reached Tessa's house, she broke down in tears. She did not tell her about the threats Sophia made, but she told her about Sean hooking up with Sophia in the past years. She was heartbroken and hurt.

Eventually, she mustered up the courage to go back to Stacey's. Surprisingly, everything of hers was just where she had left it. When she opened the door, she ran into Stacey, and all Stacey said was, "I was going to throw you out but luckily for you, my cousin begged me to give you another chance. You should be glad she is in town. She saved your ass from being homeless." Then she walked off. Sequoia knew that was not a kind gesture from Sophia; she was deliberately manipulating her life. She did not trust her one bit and she knew she had to find somewhere else to live before Sophia ruined her life any more than she did.

That night, Sequoia thought about her next action. She did not know how long Sophia would be in town and what other plans she had for her. The best course of action would be to leave the state and move as far away as possible. That way, she would not be able to destroy her life anymore. She had no choice but to use the loan for school, to leave this town; school would have to wait. She sighed deeply realizing all she was going to leave behind: her friends, work, and Sean.... Weeks had passed since her meeting with Sophia and her breakup with Sean. He respected her boundaries and so whenever they saw each other at work, they just passed by each other like strangers.

Sequoia found an apartment in another state in the country area. All she needed to do was get her affairs in order, buy her plane ticket and leave. She did not tell any of her friends of her plans to leave. She wanted to get Sonya's burial out of the way first. Then she would break the news to them. "Do we finally have a funeral date yet?" Sequoia asked her friends. "Yes, we do. Mr. Ebanks visited Sonya's husband and offered to pay the whole funeral expense. He was so happy." Sonya did not have much of a family and the few people she had were barely making a living, so it was difficult financially for Calvin, her husband, to pay for the funeral. Sequoia and the others had contributed what they could, but it was not enough.

"Oh, wow that's great," Sequoia said flatly. "Yes, it is. I am glad we are finally going to lay her to rest. That Sean is a real gentleman. He heard the whispers around here about how Calvin was struggling to pay for her funeral, and he took it upon himself to help. God bless his soul," Marge said. "Amen!" Tessa added as she side eyed Sequoia who acted uninterested.

"Sequoia, I want to retire and leave this place, but I do not want to leave you two girls here. I really want you to go back to school, do some studies and leave this God forsaken place. It is not for young folks like you with such bright minds." "Aww thanks Marge, we are working on it; do not worry. Right Sequoia?" She had to nudge Sequoia's arm to get her attention as she was staring off into space. "Um... yeah sure," she answered quickly. "Good. I will leave you two now... got to go clean that break room on the third floor before Jack pisses his pants."

They laughed and watched as she disappeared around a corner. "Sequoia.... What is up with you? You seem distant. Want to talk about it?" "I am fine Tessa...

just have a lot to deal with right now." "You mean Sean and Ashley?" "Ye… wait what…. What about Sean and Ashley?" She looked at Tessa with a wide stare. "Oh, I thought you noticed... they have been getting really close... everyone has been whispering about it." "Like how close?" "Well... I saw them leave work together in his car a couple of times... and some people say they saw them going into a restaurant together. Look, Sequoia, do not worry about it. Just forget about them."

"Hmmm." Sequoia said softly as she zoned out into her own thoughts. She had been in such a dark mood lately; she never realized that Ashley and Sean had become close. Now that she had thought about it, she remembered seeing them in his office laughing and smiling a couple of days ago. She then shook the image from her head.

CHAPTER THIRTEEN

It was finally the day of the funeral.... It was crowded but an incredibly sad day. After they finished at the graveside, the trio walked to a nearby tree where they conversed. Sean then came over to meet them under the tree and offered his condolences, after which he asked to speak with Sequoia alone. She agreed and they walked just a few feet away from Marge and Tessa.

"How are you holding up?" he asked, having a concerned look in his eyes. "I am fine," she replied as she looked over his shoulders to see Ashley dressed in full black waiting by his car. She was talking with his chauffeur. "I don't want to keep you waiting." As she spoke, she gestured to Ashley. He turned briefly and looked back at her. "Sequoia, it's not what you think, okay?" "Sean, it does not matter what I think. It is your life, so live it." He sighed and brushed his hair back. "I miss you Sequoia and I love you enough to respect your decisions. But I will always be here if you need me." He squeezed her arm briefly. Before she could reply, he walked off towards Ashley. She felt dumbstruck as emotions engulfed her.

"Hey there stranger," Ashley said as he approached her. "Hi there," he said flatly. "So, my car is at the mechanic's. My sister dropped me off with the intention of picking me up afterwards, but her son felt sick, and they had to go to the doctor..." "Is this your way of asking for a ride?" "Um... yes please if you don't mind." She gave him puppy dog eyes.

"Okay no problem. Where to?" "Ashbury Road." He opened the door for her, and she got in the car. Before he went in, he looked back to where Sequoia was. She gave him a sullen look as he entered the car. "It was a great funeral," Ashley said. "Yeah, it was. She had a big turn out." "Definitely..." There was a long pause as Sean's mind had drifted to the love of his life.

He wanted to grab her arm and whisk her away in his car, to a place far away from the hurt and pain, but he could not. She was too pissed at him to even have a decent conversation.

"So...." Sophia slid closer to him and placed her hand on his chest. She then whispered in his ear. "I would love some company at my place. I have a Jacuzzi that you would love. We could have a fun-filled evening... all your desires would come true." She kissed his cheek as her hand slowly fell to his crotch. But he chuckled to himself before removing her hand from his body. "Ashley, you are an incredibly attractive lady. As tempting as your request is, I must decline." "Are you sure? I mean, a guy like you must have desires too." "Yes, I do... but those desires can only be met by one person. The one who holds my heart and sorry my dear, but that is not you." She froze in disappointment for a few seconds. "Keep telling yourself that, Mr. Ebanks, but when you change your mind, I will be waiting." "I doubt that. Have a good night."

The car stopped, and they were at her place. She gave him a sensual wink before exiting the vehicle. Sean and his bodyguards drove off as she made her way to her doorsteps. "Didn't take you long to move on..." Sophia whispered to herself as she watched Sean from her tinted window. "Let's go Mr. Wesley," she said to her chauffeur. "Yes Ma'am," he replied as he pulled onto the road.

Weeks after the funeral, Tessa suddenly broke some news to Sequoia and Marge while they were in the break room. "My parents finally reached out to me after all these years. They apologized for cutting me off and offered to fund my full university fee to study marine biology, only if I came back home to Iowa." She sounded excited as she cried. They all congratulated her and showed their gratitude. "So, does that mean they are going to accept Todd as your boyfriend?" Sequoia questioned. "Well... fiancé now!" She revealed a nice diamond ring on her left hand. "OMG! when did this happen?" Sequoia said shocked.

"It happened the night Sonya died. I felt so bad and crushed that I could not bring myself to tell you all. I wanted to wait until after the funeral. It just did not seem right, you know, celebrating our engagement when we were mourning." "That's understandable, hun," Sequoia said. "We understand and we are happy for you," Marge said with a sincere smile. "Thanks! So yes, my parents also reached out to Todd and gave him a sincere apology. My dad already lined up a job for him there as a contractor. So, he will still be doing what he loves, but with a better pay." "Wow, so it's decided then, you're leaving?" Sequoia voiced.

"Yes, I am.... I am sorry..." "Hun, do not be sorry for living your dreams. You deserve it child. Besides, you and Todd have been through a lot together," Marge sympathized. Tessa sniffed back the tears. "I will miss you girl but when an opportunity knocks at your door, you have to take it. Your parents were wrong in the first place for disowning their only child, just because they did not like Todd for who he was. I am glad they finally came to their senses," Marge spoke firmly with sympathy in her eyes.

"Yeah, me too. Thanks guys. I do not know how I will wake up every day without you all around, but I will try. You all have been the best thing that ever happened to me since I moved here or ran away if you want to put it that way." While Tessa spoke, she placed her hand briefly on her heart.

They laughed. "But honestly, after Tiffany left and Sonya died, it was becoming too much for me. Every day, I woke up wondering if I was going to lose anyone else and I hated the feeling. This place just keeps reminding me that I lost two great friends and I know I still have you both, but it scares me to imagine my life without you all. I know it sounds ironic because I am going to leave, but that is just how it is."

"Darling, we understand you completely. I told you both I am ready to retire once you both get the heck out of this place. I am happy for you. Just keep in touch," Marge added. "It was a pleasure getting to know you, Tessa. You have been such a great friend, and we will always remember you... so do not dare forget us!" Sequoia finally said. They laughed. "I will not. I want to have a last dinner with you both this weekend before I leave," Tessa added.

"Definitely," Marge said. "Perfect, we would love that, hun," Sequoia said with a smile, but deep down she felt unhappy about Tessa's departure. They spent the next several minutes talking about Tessa's new adventure. Even though Marge was happy for Tessa, Sequoia knew deep down that Marge was going to be sad. She had lost so many friends and most recently, her dearest and oldest friend. She knew if she told them now that she was also planning to leave soon, it would devastate her, so she decided to delay her departure a while longer. That way, Marge would not feel abandoned all at once.

CHAPTER FOURTEEN

It had been a week since Tessa left and things seemed so odd. It was just her and Marge left. She was sitting alone in the lobby after work waiting for Marge when Sean walked up to her. All eyes were glued to them. She looked around, uneasy in the chair, as she quietly tried to plead with him to leave her alone, but he refused to until she agreed to go with him somewhere. She had no choice with all the loud whispers and the intensifying stares. When she was about to leave with him, Marge appeared from the elevator.

"Let me just tell Marge I am leaving," she said to him. He stepped aside for her. Before she could whisper into Marge's ear she said, "It is okay my child, go ahead. That was long overdue." She gave her a mischievous smile that left Sequoia confused. He took her to one of their favorite spots — a hilltop view that overlooked the city. It was only the two of them, no bodyguards, and no chauffeurs. He helped her out of the car, and she leaned back against the railing to face him. "We have been over this Sean, what..." "Just please, hear me out. You do not have to talk, just listen, that is all I ask of you."

"Okay." "I know you ended things with me a month ago because you thought I was not being completely honest with you, which I was not. Yes, Sophia and I used to hook up for fun but that was all it was. I never once fell for her. She always wanted more than a fling. She used to beg me to make us exclusive, but I turned her down and told her if she kept bringing back this 'us' topic, this thing between us would stop and so she complied. The last time we hooked up was a year and a half ago, and that was the last time. I told her this hooking up thing was over because I found out she was obsessed with me."

He ran his hand through his hair as he paced slowly back and forth. "I found out about her obsession with me after we hooked up at one of her mansions in Baltimore a couple of years ago. She was in the shower when I grew restless and decided to stretch my legs. I was randomly looking through the room when I accidentally knocked over her purse and some stuff fell out. I was putting it all back when I saw this small black book and a pen stuck to the side. I was curious so I went through it and that is when I saw all my past business meetings that I went to, all listed out, including the time and place. She knew we only hooked up when we both were in the same place, city, state, or town. I did not just take a plane randomly to meet her. So, all along, she was somehow retrieving information about my meetings so she could fly ahead and then pretend as if she were there for business also. Later, I also learned that she used to sabotage some of my previous relationships."

"Weren't you suspicious before when she showed up at all the places you were?" "No, because that is the thing... she made sure to not be in all the places I was at the time. But she knew of all my meetings, and she chose which places she would go to. I confronted her about it, and she confessed. So, I walked away and never looked back in her direction. I also found the snitch she paid, who was feeding her information and I reprimanded him for it." "So how do you know that she did not follow you here to New York? I mean your parents' party was all the way in Singapore."

"I am making a huge investment in your workplace, Sequoia; your company wants to use my tech in promoting a new business launch. It was in the papers so no one could miss that and surely not Sophia." "I guess." "Anyways, when I met you at the house party, I felt a connection. I am not going to lie, yes, I hooked up with a couple of women in that period before I came here to invest in the company you happened to work at. But after I ran into you again, I knew I had to have you for myself. This time, I never hooked up with anyone else. I know that being a hot, sexy billionaire like myself will always get the female's attention, but I just wanted your attention. Sequoia, I am in love with you."

She felt her breath stop at his words. "A guy like me does not love easily, trust me... you are the only woman I have ever been in love with. You are different from all the women I have been with. You do not pretend to be someone you are not around me and you speak your mind. I love those things about you. How humble, beautiful, smart, and kind you are. You never ask me for anything and when I even try to give you stuff, you do not take it. Sequoia please, just give me another chance to make it right with you."

Before she could respond, he pulled her close to his chest and gave her a passionate kiss. It was intense and bittersweet at the same time. Sequoia could feel her emotions spiraling, as the heat spread throughout her body. In the moment, she did not fight his kiss or touch; she wanted it just as bad. When his soft lips strayed to kiss her neck, she felt a small jolt run through her body. She knew if it continued, there would be no turning back and this would be unfair to him since she had made up her mind. Reluctantly, she pushed him away as she tried to catch her breath. She took a few steps back and met his worried gaze.

She then let out a big sigh and looked away from his gaze. Inside, she felt like she was tearing up, as she wanted to tell him, *yes, I forgive you*, but after what Sophia threatened her with, she could not risk that. "Sean, I can't be with you, and I am sorry." She knew those words hurt him more than how it hurt her. He looked disappointed but he just gave her a peck on her cheeks and pulled away. "I will always respect your wishes, darling. I am sorry for the pain I caused you, and I hope one day you can forgive me."

She nodded and not long after, they headed to her house. He dropped her off at the usual spot but before he drove off, he called out to her through the window. "I am leaving for Dubai tomorrow, and I will not be back for at least a month or so. Take care of yourself and if you need me, I am one call away. Goodbye, Sequoia." Before she could reply, he sped off. She could not believe she had just made the love of her life drive away and there was a chance she might never see him again. Tears filled her eyes as she walked silently to her house.

***

Sophia watched attentively through the one-way mirror at her guest, who was tied to a chair and blindfolded. "Please who are you? What do you want… Please let me go," Ashley pleaded and begged. "You know what to do," Sophia said to a thick tall guy nearby. He nodded and entered the room where she was. "Please, you don't have to do this… please!" The tall guy removed a sharp knife from his side pocket. He walked slowly behind her, ignoring her cries. He gripped her head and pulled it back and before she knew it, the knife was at her throat cutting through her skin. Her screams continued briefly and then it stopped as her lifeless body slammed in the chair, blood dripping all over. An evil smile spread across Sophia's face as she looked down on the picture on her phone. It was a picture of Sequoia going into Sean's car.

"See my dear, I told you what would happen if you disobeyed me. Now you will pay." The next day, after the bus dropped Sequoia at the usual bus stop, she walked down towards Zenith Capital Industries. She was almost at the entrance when someone wearing a hoodie and shades grabbed her tightly by her hand and pulled her away. "My child, what are you doing here? Did you not receive my voice messages! I have been calling you since morning." It was Marge and she looked frightened.

Sequoia then took out her phone that was switched off. She tried turning it on, but her battery was dead, because she had forgotten to charge it. "My phone must have died... Marge what is it? What is wrong?" "Follow me now. We do not have much time."

Sequoia was confused as she followed her hurriedly to a secluded spot. "Some police officers were here earlier, looking for you. I left them with Mike, waiting by the lobby for you."

"What... why?" "You know my husband is a retired policeman, but he goes by the station every morning to do some volunteer work. He sometimes helps with cases too. Anyway, he overheard them calling out your name about some murder. So, he pretended to be curious about the case and they told him that Ashley was murdered last night! They found her body in her car parked outside, with her throat slashed." "OMG! That's inhumane. But Marge, what does that have to do with me?" "He said they found some papers in her possession about you! Something about you being an undocumented immigrant, who had committed a murder some years ago!"

Sequoia felt dizzy and queasy, "OMG." "... they also found DNA evidence at the crime scene that links you to Ashley's murder!" Marge walked over to her and shook her. "Child, get it together because I know you are not a murderer, but with all that evidence pointed against you, in their eyes that is a motive…. You need to run now! I do not want you in jail, baby girl." She broke down in tears as she spoke. "This cannot be happening! Shit! It must have been Sophia… she did this to me Marge, but I do not…"

"Child, forget about that. Just leave so you can figure this out and get your name cleared…. Here take this…" Marge handed her an envelope with money. "It is not much but it can take you far from here. Do not let them catch you. You hear me!" "I am sorry, Marge... I really am... I..." "It's okay just go!" "I have a backpack in my locker which has some important things I would need to take with me. Is there any way you could get it for me?" Marge nodded and made a phone call. After a few minutes, she disappeared and returned with her backpack. Sequoia wiped her tears as she hugged her briefly. "Thank you for everything, Marge."

"Take care…. my child, until we meet again." She put on her backpack and walked away. One thing she learned from her mother while they were on the run, was to always have a backup plan and a place to hide, because you never know when you have to just disappear. Luckily, she had withdrawn a hefty sum of money a few days ago and stashed it in her bag in preparation for her relocation out of New York. It did not take her long to hop on a bus that was headed to the train station. She knew where she was going to... Queens-bury at a homeless shelter. That was one of the places she and her mom went to hide for some time. Even though it was known to be a homeless shelter, the owner had a side operation, in which persons who were on the run could hide out for a while, if you paid a 'fee'. She knew that if she could make it there, staying there would buy her some time until she could change her identity again. While she was on the train, she somehow knew that Sophia was behind her downfall. She also figured out that the probable reason the police did not come looking for her at her house was because, the address she used on all her documents, as well as the one on file at her workplace, was false.

CHAPTER
FIFTEEN

After a five-hour drive, she arrived in Queens-bury and made her way to a convenience store where she picked up a couple of snacks, hair dye and scissors. She used a public bathroom to cut her hair and dye it black with streaks of red. It was now her new look. She then found the homeless shelter at the same abandoned building it was before. The lady in charge was a bit hesitant to offer her sanctuary, but after Sequoia showed her a small tattoo of a code written in mandarin, she accepted the cash and happily welcomed her.

There were forty other people living there, including children. Sequoia spread her blanket on the small bed that was in the corner of the room and used her bagpack as a pillow. She had to ditch her previous attire and put on something a bit duller, so that she could blend in more. "Hi there, welcome to paradise. I am Lucy." She turned to see an average sized brunette smiling warmly at her; she looked she was in her early thirties. Sequoia returned her welcome with a brief smile. "Hi, I am Sasha, nice to meet you," Sequoia replied. "Thanks. I saw you when you came in, and I thought you were lost."

"Why is that?" "Because a decent, pretty girl like you does not look homeless." "Well, I could say the same about you and some of the other people I saw here earlier." She chuckled. "That's true, but you kind of stand out." "Is that so?" "Yep, but I guess because you are new, I see you in that way. Over time, I am sure you will blend in once I get used to you being around."

Sequoia gave her a kind smile as she removed another blanket from her bagpack. "Well, I am not sure how I feel about that statement since I might not be sticking around for long." "Hmmm," Lucy gave a sly smile. "That's what I said to myself six months ago but hey, who's counting?!" "Probably Alexa," she said as she gestured to a speaker by Lucy's bedside. They both laughed in unison. "I like you, Sasha. I think we are going to get along just fine." "I think so too," she replied, giving her a kind smile.

"Anyways, if you want, I can show you a good place to take a shower." "Really... what happened to the shower stalls at the back?" "Have you been here before?" Sequoia shrugged her shoulders. "Um..." "It is okay. I am not one to judge but anyways, those showers have been overrun with rats, and it is pretty nasty in there. Heard some people say since this new guy started running things, the place is not what it used to be."

"I see. So where is this anti-rat shower located?" she whispered. "I found a place close by. It is a rundown apartment that has been abandoned for years. There is a secret entrance I use to get in. Surprisingly, the showers on the ground floor still work." "And you're the only one who knows about it?" "No, I told two other women here. We try to keep it a secret because if everyone found out, they would use it and then we would definitely get caught." "Hmm sounds nice. When do you all normally go?" "In the evenings, like around 6 p.m. You can join us if you like. Just let me know."

"Okay, I will take it into consideration." "Okay no problem. Anyways, I think I have bored you enough. It was nice meeting you Sasha... if you need anything, I am right by that wall."

She gestured to her bed close to where they stood. "Thanks again. Bye." Sequoia spent the next several days hanging out with Lucy. They had grown somewhat close. It was nice having a little friend to talk to. In the evenings, they would join the little bonfires and socialize with some of the other people living there. One late evening, they decided to watch the sunset from on top of their building. Both girls were seated on a blanket, drinking beer, and eating fish N' chips.

"So, can I ask how you ended up here?" Sequoia managed to ask. "Well, I got involved with the wrong people. I had a boyfriend, Tony, who ran a drug business which I also got involved in. I was good with numbers, so he trusted me to balance the books and do all the monetary work. Things were going well until we did business with some Latinos. Things went sideways and they came to our place and..."

She gulped hard as a look of sadness overwhelmed her. "...it was a blood bath. I managed to escape, but Tony died..." She paused for a few seconds, to sniff back the tears and then she cleared her throat. "I barely made it out alive. I got shot three times — here, here, and here." She pointed to the healed scars on her body. "I dragged my bloodied self into the road and waved down a car that took me to the hospital. They saved my life. Next day when I woke up, the police were at the hospital asking me all sorts of questions. I lied to them about the reason I was at Tony's place.... I told them I was there against my will, as a part of their human trafficking ring. I told them a lot of bullcrap to get them off my case and they believed me. One day, the nurse brought me a bundle of flowers with a note attached. When I read it, my heart leaped.... it was a warning from an anonymous person, telling me to run because the Latinos were coming for me.... I had no choice but to leave. I had some money stashed away and so I left the country; that was in Belize. I forged some fraudulent documents that allowed me to stay under the radar, but it was not enough to get a decent job. So, here I am."

"Wow! I am so sorry to hear. I cannot imagine the hardships you must have faced to be here." "Hardships indeed, but hey, that's just life right? You can either make it devour you or you devour it instead. I chose to survive." She took a big bite of her fish, and it made a crunchy sound. This made Sequoia smile. "That's true." She sipped her beer as a brief moment of silence lingered. "So, what about you... what's your story??" Lucy finally asked.

"Um, my story isn't as exciting as yours." Lucy laughed. "That's okay my friend... in life there has to be a balance." "True. But anyways, um... I used to work as an accountant, and I laundered a lot of money from my workplace. The company hired this auditor who was close to exposing my little secret, but I had a head start before they could take any legal action. I just did not think prison would suit me well." "I don't think so either." They both laughed and spent the rest of the evening talking. A week later, two rough looking men came into the shelter to extort a few people. "Are they allowed to do that? Why won't anyone stop them?" Sequoia asked in shock, as she stared at what was unfolding before her eyes. Lucy quickly pulled her to the side and behind a crowd of onlookers. "I do not know how long ago you were here, but things are not what they used to be. This new gang has been running the town for the last few years. They are called the 'Tiger gang'. I heard their boss threatened our boss about exposing this little side hustle if they did not agree to the extortion. They come here at least once a month, even though she pays them..."

She gestured to the lady that oversaw the operation. She was the one Sequoia had paid the funds to, in order to get the refuge, she needed. "They still make trouble by going around and taking our food. We just give them what they want because we do not want any trouble. Their leader is heartless, and they will kill anyone who puts up a fight or does not want to cooperate with them." "Seriously? There are two of them and forty of you. There are so many things lying down here that could be used as weapons." "Are you crazy?? They have guns and there are more of them spread across this town and neighboring cities but only two of them come every month. They are not to be messed with so please just stay put." Sequoia rolled her eyes in disgust as she watched them slap a guy in his face for his canned tuna.

"Cover your face up some more. You cannot let them see you." As she spoke, she tried pulling the hoodie some more over Sequoia's face. "Wait what... why? Do not tell me they know all forty people's faces here!?" "Not necessarily... just new females or the ones that entice them." "Entice?? What do they do?" She looked into Lucy's fearful eyes. She swallowed hard. "They have their way with them sometimes." "OMG... that is... wait, did they do that to you?" Lucy nodded sadly at her. "That is disgusting. I won't stand for..."

"Shhhh, shhhh, they are coming to our side. Just keep your head down behind these people until they have passed."

Hesitantly, she did as she was told. She could smell the masculinity on them as they came closer. "Hi Lucy, long time no see." She heard a gruff voice speak. Sequoia tried to keep her head down while trying to get a side glance.

Lucy's body tensed up as one of the gangsters walked over to her and stroked her face. "You look good Lucy. What do you say? You and I can take a walk over to one of the empty rooms." "Please... not today. Please," she heard Lucy whispering. "Oh, come on, girl." He pulled her but her body stiffened as she tried to resist. Sequoia felt uneasy and a déjà vu feeling came over her, and so she intervened. "She said no, asshole!" She jumped between them. "Well, look what we have here. Fresh meat and she is damn pretty, too. "We are going to have a treat," one gangster with an orange cap on his head said.

"No, please leave her alone. I will go with you," Lucy pleaded but they just pushed her aside and dragged Sequoia away. She did not even put up much of a fight because she had devised a plan for them. They took her to one of the empty rooms in the abandoned building, and one of the guys held her arms tightly from behind. "Oh, you're not even a fighter, huh baby?" One of the guys spoke as he unbuckled his pants, but Sequoia just smiled. "Oh, you will have a fight. I promise." After he unbuckled his pants, he gestured to the other guy to force her to her knees. "See this pipe here, I need it cleaned as a whistle." He had a disgusting laugh as he licked his lips. "My pleasure." Sequoia pretended to lower her head as she slipped the knife that was up her sleeve into her palm. In a swift motion, she stabbed his foot. The knife went straight through his sneakers. He cried in anguish and stumbled backwards. The other gangster, who realized what had taken place, grabbed his gun from his waist. "You're dead bitch!" he yelled. But luckily for her, the gun jammed and this gave her the opportunity to seek cover by a nearby rusted locker. While the gangster was busy trying to reload back the gun, she searched for a weapon. A loose brick laid few feet a way, which she quickly grabbed. With all her strength she, threw it in his direction. The brick hit the side of his head with such force, he lost his balance and he became briefly disoriented. The gun slid from his hand. Without hesitation, she grabbed the gun. She shot him twice, once in each leg debilitating him.

By the time she turned her attention back to the gangster in the orange cap, he had already regained his composure and he caught her off guard, knocking the gun from her hand; it slid across the room. He then landed a few blows in her abdomen, which caused her to fall to the ground. While she was on the ground, she tried to reach for the gun, but he grabbed her legs and pulled her towards him. Luckily, she spotted a piece of shattered glass and grabbed it just in time. The guy flipped her on her back violently and hovered over her.

"You are mine!" Without hesitation, she stabbed him in his neck with the glass shard. Blood spurted out as he held his neck and gasped. She pushed his body aside and ran from the room. "Sequoia!" Lucy ran to meet her after she emerged out of the room. "Oh my God, are you okay??" Sequoia's face was bloodied, her lip and face were bleeding, and she had several bruises over her body. "I am sorry. I had to defend myself and so I fought them and stabbed the leader. I think he is dead! I…" "OMG! Sequoia you must leave. Once they find out what you did, they are going to come for you. You must go! Now!" Sequoia hugged her briefly and said, "I am sorry." "I know you were just trying to protect me… stay safe." So, Sequoia grabbed her bagpack and ran from the building without looking back. She knew all eyes were on her, but she did not care. The only thing she cared about was her survival.

CHAPTER SIXTEEN

Sequoia stopped at the building that Lucy showed her and cleaned up. She managed to rid herself of the blood stains, but her eye, jaw and lip were still bruised. She then took a bus to a nearby town. She walked aimlessly for hours until she came upon a junkyard. It was getting late, so she crawled through a hole that she found in the fence into the yard. An old RV caught her eye and that is where she spent the night. Inside the RV was dusty and old but she had seen worse. There was a bed in the corner, so she spread her blanket on the dusty mattress and fell asleep.

The next morning, she woke up to the sound of a muffled voice. She looked through the blinds to see a girl, not older than a teenager, talking on her cellphone. The dust from the blinds irritated her sinuses so Sequoia could not help but sneeze. She let go of the blinds just as the girl looked her way. "Hello... Is someone in there??" The girl inched closer to the RV, but Sequoia remained quiet. "Okay, I am calling the police." "Wait No! No!" Sequoia opened the door with her hands up in the air. "Don't call the police. I was just leaving." "People always fall for that trick. I am Candy by the way... what is a pretty girl like you doing in that old thing?" "I... um... just needed somewhere to crash for the night. I will be on my way." "I know I am seventeen but that does not mean I am stupid. You are hiding from someone."

"Look, kid, please just..." "Hey, it is none of my business, okay lady. I am just pointing out the obvious." "Whatever. What is a seventeen-year-old doing in a junkyard anyways?" "Do not worry about that. You have your reasons, I have mine." Sequoia scoffed. "You look hungry. I have a sandwich and a bottle of coke in my backpack if you want it." "No thanks, I am good." But a loud growl erupted from

Sequoia's belly. Candy laughed. "Okay fine, hand me the damn thing."

She watched as Candy opened her bag revealing not only the snacks, but a Math and an English textbook. Sequoia took the snacks and sat on the steps of the RV. "So can I ask why you are ditching school?" Candy gave her the stink eye. "Come on! It's not like you're ever going to see me again... who am I going to tell?" Candy leaned her back against the RV as she sighed. "My boyfriend was supposed to meet me here."

"What? Of all the places, he chose a junkyard. How old is he?" "It is not what you think, okay. He is eighteen. He asked me to ditch school today so we could spend time together today." Her cheeks flushed and Sequoia knew exactly what that meant. "Kid, I am a grown adult so you can say the word. You and I both know that you are not just going to hang out." "Okay fine... we were going to 'do it'. It was going to be my first time." "Do it where? In a junkyard?" "I guess... we found an old RV over on the east side. We got inside cleaned up a couple of days ago. But he is not answering his phone. I called him like a thousand times."

"How long have you been together?" "One year." "Does he live close by?" "Yes, just a couple blocks away but I cannot go visit him at his house. He lives with his mom and she and my mom have a feud, so they do not want us dating." "So, you skipped school to be with him... okay then. Does he love you?" "Of course, he does."

"How do you know that?" "That's a dumb question... because he told me so." "Look kid, I am not one to judge but if he loves you that much, he shouldn't ask you to skip school just to 'hang out'... a guy who really cares for you would not make you miss out on a chance of bettering yourself in life, just so you can have sex. I am sorry but that is just how I see it. And your first time should not be in a junkyard in an old dusty van. It should be romantic and relaxing." As she spoke, she thought of Sean.

"Because that moment is a special time in your life; you will always remember it. And if he cannot respect you enough to wait for better circumstances to arrive, then he is not worth giving yourself to. Also, in regard to the family feud, you have two options: you can either listen to your mom and stay away from him, or you do not. Sometimes, mothers have their reasons for telling you these things. It is not because she does not want you to live your life, but she does not want you to ruin it also." "Wow! You sound just like my mom," Candy said with sincerity. "But if you decide to ignore your mom's advice and do what you want, just remember every action has consequences... and the question is, are you ready to deal with or face those consequences.... Just think about those consequences. Only you can know what is best for you Candy." A few seconds of silence passed before she spoke. "Thank you... that is the best advice I have ever received. I guess I have been hearing my mom preach to me so much, I never realized it was the exact thing she was telling me."

"Sometimes, you just need to hear the same thing from someone else... that's when you get the wakeup call," she chuckled. "Yeah, I guess." "You're welcome." "Well, I can still make it to school. I will just be two hours late. I am going to have to find an excuse when my mom finds out." "You will think of something." "Yeah, I will. See you later." "Goodbye." The day went by quickly, and Sequoia decided that once night came, she would leave for the train station. She had made contact earlier with her 'supplier' who confirmed that her documents were ready; all she had to do was get a ride and meet at the spot with the payment. It was now nightfall, and she was about to leave the RV, when she heard running footsteps and then a loud bang on the door.

"Hey! Hey lady!" It was Candy and she sounded nervous. Sequoia opened the door to see Candy breathless and shaking. She was drenched in sweat. "Hey, what is wrong? Are you okay?" "You... need... to..." She gasped for air as she tried to catch her breath. "You need to leave now. Some bad men are coming for you." "Wait what??? Why?? Who is coming??"

"I was over at my best friend's house, telling her about my boyfriend and her big brother overheard me telling her about this Indian looking chick that I met at the junkyard. When he questioned me about you, I thought he was simply curious but then I heard him telling someone on the phone that they 'found the bitch who stabbed Malcolm.' They are coming for you. I am so sorry!" "Shit! Shit!" Sequoia knew exactly who they were. When Lucy told her they had a large network of gangs that stretched across different towns, she never took it seriously until now. "Go now, Candy! Leave before they get here!" "What about you??? They will kill you..." "Do not worry about me. Take care of yourself. Go now!" Candy cried as she ran hesitantly into the darkness and disappeared.

Sequoia headed towards the hole in the fence but was stopped in her tracks by a group of men coming her way. "Oh damn!" They saw her and immediately opened fire at her. She ran away just in time and took cover behind the cars that worked as the perfect shield. She quickly and cautiously made her way through the junkyard. "I can't see anything!" One of the men shouted. "Use the damn flashlight and shut your mouth." They fired a couple more shots at anything that moved. She needed to find a way to distract them from coming in her direction, so she picked up a nearby stone and threw it in the opposite direction. She heard when they ran towards it shouting. "She is over there!"

She used that opportunity to enter one of the cars and slid under it just in time as the men came back to that side of the junkyard. She heard their boots and the clicks of their guns as they searched but never found her. She laid on the cold, grassy ground under an old sports car for hours. She never even realized she had drifted off into sleep, until the rays of the morning sun hit her. The men had left hours ago. She came out of her hiding place cautiously and swiftly made her way from the junkyard. She took a bus that dropped her off on one of those dusty roads surrounded by bushes. The sun was hot, and she felt dirty as she walked in the sun trying to hitchhike a ride. Eventually, a nice couple, Mr. and Mrs. Richardson, who drove an RV, stopped by to give her a ride. They were headed to Wisconsin; a fifteen-hour drive. They had their thirteen-year-old daughter and eight-year-old son with them as well. They all seemed pleasant except their daughter who just ignored Sequoia's handshake. She went to the spare bunk bed where she threw herself on and not long after she fell asleep, hoping that better days lie ahead.

CHAPTER SEVENTEEN

Sequoia was suddenly awoken by Mrs. Richardson; they were going to spend the night at a motel, and they had paid for her room at no cost to her. Sequoia had initially declined their offer, but they insisted. So, for the first in a long while, she was able to have a good and refreshing shower. Morning came and they were back on the road again. Mrs. Richardson confided in Sequoia that her daughter, Tina, was not happy about their move to Wisconsin and was lashing out. Sequoia agreed to talk to her to see if she could help. Tina was lying in her bunk bed, reading a book. "Hi Tina, it is me again Sasha. What are you reading?"

"A book, obviously." She did not even look up at Sequoia. "I know but what's it about?" "Why do you care? It is not like you are going to read it anyway."

"Well, I love books and I have read quite a few. So, try me. What is it called?" "It is called the *Restless Redemption*. It is about..." she started to say angrily. "A girl who sought redemption from her parents, because they thought she was the one responsible for the murder of her two-year-old brother who had cerebral palsy." This captured Tina's attention as she closed the book and looked up at Sequoia.

"You have read it before?" "Yeah, it's a pretty deep book kid... that main character, Tatiana, she is a real badass." "Yes, I said the same thing too! What do you think about Roger, the guy that she met in chapter three at the gas station?" "Was he the one with the red hair who always wore that green sweater with a bunny on it?" "Yes, that's him!" "At first, I thought he was sweet, but I think he is a creep with a lot of emotional baggage."

"I know right! He is such a douche bag. I am almost finished with the book, but I am so scared of the ending. I just feel Suzan, Tatiana's bestie is going to die." "Well... I do not want to spoil the surprise because you are in for a real treat but just remember these words, 'I lied, cried and now I survived'." "What does that mean?" she said, looking confused. "No spoilers, remember. I will say no more." Sequoia pretended to zip her mouth shut and she laughed. "So, Tina... if you do not mind me asking, what is up with you? Your mom said you have withdrawn yourself ever since the move?"

"Ugh... I just hate that we have to move all the way across the state and leave my friends behind. It is going to suck. I do not see why we have to move." "Did they tell you why they are moving?" "My dad got some new job that makes more money." "Well, I know the feeling... I was a little older than you when my mom moved me from Grenada." "Oh shit! Sorry excuse my language. That must have been awful." "Yes, it was. At least you grew up here, but I lived most of my life in the Caribbean. I had a lot of friends I was attached to, so letting them go was hard. I was pissed at my mom too, but I knew deep down she had her reasons. I knew it must be for the greater good."

"But didn't you miss your friends?" "Yes, I did, but staying mad at my mother was not going to let her move back home... so I had to find ways to cope... I did things that would keep me busy, and things that I loved such as painting and writing stories. Eventually, I became used to living here and when I grew older, I made some new friends." Sequoia reminisced about her friends back at the workplace as she spoke.

"Those friends became better than my old friends back at home and now I cannot imagine what my life would have been like if I had never moved here. I would not have met such wonderful people who made me feel at home. So, Tina, I know moving sucks and you miss your friends but just try to look at it differently. Would you rather your dad left home to work indefinitely in another state, and you only saw him once a month or year?" "No, I would not," she spoke sadly. "And why is that?" "Because he is my dad. He should be by my side, and I love him."

"Exactly! So those are the things your dad took into consideration before he made this decision. I am sure he could have decided to move all by himself and leave you both with just your mother. But instead, he chose to take you with him because he loves you. This new job, do you think it is just for himself? It is for you and your brother's wellbeing as well. He wants to make sure his little princess and his prince have everything they need to survive in this world. He wants you to grow up knowing he did everything he could to give you a decent life. So just cut them some slack and give them a chance."

She nodded as she sniffed back a tear. "Thank you. When you put it that way, I feel so dumb and selfish." "That's okay... sometimes we all have to be dumb and selfish until someone wise comes along and shows us the way." They talked for a few extra minutes, after which she went up front to where the Richardson's were. "Thank you so much!" As soon as Sequoia passed through the curtain, Mrs. Richardson hugged her. "I would hug you too darling, but I can't take my hands off the wheel," Mr. Richardson managed to say.

"We had a camera installed in the RV years ago after we had a minor 'incident'. So, we were listening to the live feed. I am sorry we did not disclose this to you before." She gestured to her tablet that showed the live feed of the back of the RV. "That is okay. I am a stranger, so I understand why you never told me." "Your words impacted her greatly; I can see it in her eyes. Thank you so much." "It was my pleasure." Hours later, they arrived in Wisconsin and Sequoia had them drop her off in a small town. She hoped that from there, she could get a bus to the city so she could meet with her contact at the arranged location.

There was an Easter day parade taking place and so it was quite congested and noisy. As Sequoia pushed through the crowds, she noticed a group of police officers up ahead in her path. They were watching the crowd attentively. She looked around and saw a nearby costume stand so she made her way over there to purchase a big hat with a bunny on top, a green T-shirt with an egg logo and a basket. She dropped her backpack in the basket and put her costume on in no time. She blended in well by pretending to dance to the music as she passed by the police officers. Once she saw an alley to her right that led to another street, she discreetly slipped from the crowd. In the alley, she stopped to take her backpack from the basket.

"What's in that bag… lady?" A male voice spoke from behind. Her heart skipped a beat as she wondered if the police officer had followed her into the alley. "Um…" she stuttered as she slowly turned around to see herself surrounded by six males and two females. She muttered to herself, *'You have got to be kidding me.'* "Look please, I don't want any trouble." "I asked, what's in the bag." "Just some clothes okay." "Well, then you wouldn't mind if we took a look." "Damn right I mind. I do not know you people so get the hell out of my way!"

She turned to leave but these strangers blocked her path. She looked towards the road at the ongoing parade, but no one was looking in her direction. "Give us the bag and you can go about your business." She chuckled briefly, "I am not giving you shit!" Two of the guys came at her but she kicked them in their chests and sent them flying on the ground. The others closed in on her and she managed to kick and punch them but she herself took blows. In the middle of the fight, one of the guys caught her off guard and used a nearby empty bottle to smack her hard on her head. It shattered into pieces, and it stunned her briefly. They seized that opportunity to pull the backpack from her frozen body and ran off into the streets. By the time she regained her composure and ran after them, they had already disappeared into the crowd. There was no use chasing after them and so all her money and old documents were gone.

She touched her throbbing head, where the glass hit her and saw a small amount of blood on her fingers. She winced in pain as she walked slowly towards the other street. She found a public bathroom by a gas station where she used to clean herself up. She made her way back onto the streets where she walked for several minutes until she came to a bar with a sign in front which said, 'WE ARE HIRING'. She had already phoned her contact and rescheduled the meeting for next week. She still had some money in her pocket from what Marge had given her, so all she had to do was to work a couple more dollars and she could make up the difference to pay for her documents.

She went inside the bar and spoke to the owner about the job, but he wanted some identification. She told him what had happened earlier, that she was robbed of her belongings but he never seemed to care and so he denied her the job. She walked out furiously from the bar. "What else could go wrong?!!" She looked in the sky as she shouted and, in a few minutes, it started to rain. She swore under her breath as she walked through the streets in the rain, aimlessly.

Several thoughts raced through her mind and suddenly, she never cared if she was wet. Her life was in shambles, and she could not be strong anymore. She cried softly to herself as she walked in the pouring rain. She had been walking for about thirty minutes when a strange car pulled up a couple of feet away from her path. She stopped and tried to blink away the pouring rain from her eyesight. The figure that stood in front of her was blurry, so she took a few more steps closer to see… Sean Ebanks was standing in front of her! She was shocked; she rubbed her eyes constantly, wondering if her mind was playing tricks on her. She stood at a standstill as he walked over to her in the pouring rain.

CHAPTER EIGHTEEN

"I think we have to stop meeting like this... I think this is the second time," he joked. "Are you really here??" she managed to say. "Yes, I am here, Sequoia," he said as he reached for her hand and used it to touch his face. "This is real, hun." "Sean..." "It is okay Sequoia... I know everything." "Everything? Sean, I doubt you know what a disaster my life has been... the awful things I have done."

"Yes, I know exactly what you have done and what you have been through, Sequoia. Or should I say Khushi Gupta..." She looked at him in shock. She opened her mouth to speak but he stopped her.

"Let me please. I know that what you told me about your mother and Al was true. Any mother would have done the same thing if they were in that position. But that does not make you or your mother a murderer. He was going to hurt you and your mother acted out in self-defense. You both were on the run not only because of what she had done, but because your green cards had expired, and you would be deported back to Grenada to a life of poverty." He paused for a bit as he inched closer.

"Sequoia, in my eyes, you and your mom were not murderers. What happened all those years ago will never change the image I have of you." "But I should have stopped her! I could have stopped her from killing him, but I could not. Instead, I just stood there," she said breaking down in tears, as the image appeared in her mind. "Yes, and anyone in shock would have done what you did, but he was going to kill you both if your mother never acted quickly. Research says that in danger, our bodies go into fight or flight mode but for mothers, especially when it comes to their young, they will always be in fight mode. Do not blame yourself. At least you were able to have a few more years with her, instead of watching your stepfather snatch her life away from you in that very instant."

"Yeah, but it is still my fault we had to run away! When he raped me, if I never told my mom then maybe she would not have done what she did. She would still be alive, and able to get the proper treatment she needed, instead of wasting away in a stranger's home. I... I..." Her voice broke down more as she tried to express her dreadful thoughts. Sean stepped swiftly towards her and cupped her chin into his soft moist palms. "Don't you dare say that! Sequoia, no one deserves to have their innocence taken away from them and then left to bear the pain alone. If I had a child and I found out his or her innocence was stolen by someone like that, I would be enraged, and I would have wanted nothing but to see that person's body lifeless before my eyes! It was not your fault; he was a monster! He made his bed; he deserves to lie in it. It is sad that your mother had an untimely demise, but it was never your fault, as it was beyond your control. Cancer respects no one and does not respect time. Cancer only takes your time. It took away the time you had with your mother, but I am sure your mother never once regretted the decision she made to save your life.

Hun, you must forgive yourself and know that you are worthy of love."

Sequoia stared at him with her tear-filled eyes as she pondered on his every word. She felt the sincerity in his words as they stared into each other's eyes briefly. Only the sound of raindrops and cars passing by could be heard.

"And what is the big deal if you both got fake documents and made a life here? That does not make you less of a person. You are just human. You did what you had to do to survive. And I know the hard choice you had to make when you were left with nothing. After living so many years on the street, you accepted what you thought was a friendly invitation from Stacey to live with her. You trusted her and she betrayed you by mistreating you. You had to live in her garage while you tried to make an honest living... Sequoia, you did nothing wrong! It was Sophia who was to blame. She meddled in your life and now because of her, you have to be on the run again.... but darling I am here to tell you... you do not have to run anymore. I know what she did to

Ashley..." "You do?" she asked as desperation and sadness filled her eyes. "Yes, I do, and it was low of her to try and pin it on you. I made sure she paid for putting you through all of this. The detectives know she was the one responsible for Ashley's death and not you." Sequoia was just speechless and shocked. He then closed in on the space between them as he stared into her sad eyes that were drenched with rain. "My lawyer sorted out everything and you are free to roam this country as you please. You deserve every right to be here just like anyone else. You are neither wanted for any murder nor are you considered illegal."

Sequoia could not believe her ears as she stared slack-jawed at him in disbelief. His words replayed in her mind. She pulled from his embrace and took a couple of steps backwards. "Sequoia, please do not do this... let me help you. All you have to do is sign some papers and you are free... free from everything and everyone — even me. You would not owe me anything... we would still go our separate ways. But please, just take this offer, I beg you."

"No! No!" She shouted at him. The rain had eased up a bit and it was now drizzling. "Sequoia, please, I..." "No, that's not what I want… Sean." "What do you mean? You can be free." "I don't want to be free… from you...." He froze at hearing her words. "I am tired of running away from my fears. I was scared to fall in love with you because I wondered why a guy like you could want a girl to like me. I was not rich, I do not have good taste in fashion, I am homeless, and I work as a housekeeper. I was too ordinary for you. At first, I never wanted to believe that you could love someone like me. But after I had the opportunity to get to know you more, my feelings for you changed. Sophia played on my insecurities, and I should have never played into her game. I feared that you would leave me just like so many people that left my life... but the more I pushed you away, the more I wanted you. Sean Ebanks, you changed me in ways that I never knew were possible and I am so deeply sorry I hid the truth from you. I am sorry I never told you about Sophia's threats and I am sorry I lied to you. The truth is, ever since I told you to walk away, I was broken into pieces; I was never whole. When you told me you were going to Dubai and I let you walk away, I felt my heart shatter into a million more pieces. I am in love with you, and I hope you can find it in your heart to give me another chance."

The rain had finally stopped, and a silence hung midair between them for a few seconds. Then Sean locked his lips on hers and kissed her passionately until they both were breathless. "Sequoia, I accept your apology and I am yours." She smiled and kissed him again. "And we are soaking wet." He pulled from her embrace and stared at his suit. "Yeah, we need to get out of these clothes." "Yes, my dear, we do. There is a hotel nearby. Let us go there." "Wait, you drove yourself?" "Oh, come on, do not treat me like that. I can help myself." "Where are your bodyguards?" He gestured to a black Subaru parked nearby, with two men in suits standing at the door. "Were they here all along?" "Yes, they were. But unlike us, they were standing under an umbrella." She laughed as they got into the car.

Once they reached the hotel, they cleaned themselves up and in a matter of seconds, they were all over each other. Sequoia pushed his naked body onto the bed as she removed her robe. She stared hungrily at his erection as she crawled towards him. She kissed his warm red lips, moved down his neck and to his chest. She played with his nipples briefly before slowly lowering her wet core onto his body. His body tensed up as they both let out a slow moan. She started rocking her hips back and forth on his manhood, as she felt it going deeper inside of her. He sucked her nipples as she rode him with a captivating power. She could feel his manhood throbbing inside of her as she moaned with pleasure. He pulled her body closer to him not wanting to be released from her grip. She rode him until they were both drenched in sweat and when they both climaxed at the same time, it felt like fireworks. They both let out a last cry as they both trembled into each other's arms. She then laid on his chest listening to both their heartbeats slowing down.

"I missed you so much," she whispered breathlessly. "And I, you." Then they drifted off into sleep. They woke up after a few hours and started talking about the events that had transpired in the last few days. "So, I am really going to be an American citizen?" "Yes, you will be my dear. My lawyer will be waiting for us at 8 a.m. sharp to sign those papers." "Thank you." She kissed him sweetly. "And I packed all your stuff from the garage into a storage container." "OMG! You did?" He nodded. "We also found out that the DNA they found at Ashley's crime scene was taken from your brush. Sophia had access to your garage with all your personal stuff."

"That bitch! I cannot believe she went that far just because of her obsession with you." "Yeah, an obsession I should have dealt with years ago." "It is not your fault. Do not beat yourself up about it... but how did you find out what happened? I mean were you not in Dubai?" "Marge called me. She said you had panicked and left your phone when you ran... I had just landed in Dubai, but I told the pilot to take me back to New York immediately! He looked at me as if I was crazy, but I was crazy... crazy in love with you. I had to find you." She laughed.

"On the return flight back to New York, I had persons of all different ranks in the police force investigating your case. I had persons investigate Ashley's murder, as well as the documents that were found concerning you. I hired someone to follow Sophia until they had the evidence, they needed to prove that she was responsible for the murder. I even had a few strings pulled from people in higher places that even Sophia had no access to, courtesy of my parents…"

"Your parents?" she looked up at him in disbelief. "Yeah, I needed all the help I could get to take down Sophia and I knew they had a lot of people in their pockets, so I reached out to them." "Weren't they shocked or hesitant to help after what happened in Singapore?" "Nope. In fact, they were cooperative. After our confrontation, they had some self-introspection at one of their 'spiritual retreats' and wanted to make amends. It was the perfect timing.

Anyways, that is how I found out what happened, and based on what you told me at my place about your past, I was able to connect the dots. By the time I landed in America, I knew exactly what had happened." "I am sorry I was so stubborn with my emotions. I should have told you the truth." "Shhh… it's okay my dear, that is in the past; 'et's focus on our future together." They kissed briefly before she spoke.

"Sean... since we are being honest about everything, there is something you should know." She eased up from his bare chest and locked eyes with him.
"What is it?" "While I was at a shelter in Queens-bury something happened..." "I know what happened." "Wait what... you know about the gang and what I did?" "Yes, I do. I met Lucy... she told me. Do not worry, I took care of that also. That gang will not be a bother to you. And the guy you stabbed did not die. He is alive and well."

"How did you…" "Trust me, it took a lot of tracking from my private investigators to find your whereabouts and eventually, they did. I told them not to rest until they found you." She chuckled softly. "Thank you for not giving up on me." "Thank you for giving us a chance…"

CHAPTER NINETEEN

"Hey, I know it's late and you probably want to sleep but I have something to tell you," Sean said as he nudged Sequoia awake. She yawned and turned onto her side facing him. "It's okay, I wasn't asleep anyways. What's on your mind?" she said attentively. He sighed heavily and sat up in bed. "So, this is probably not the right time since it's our honeymoon but I can't keep this to myself any longer. I have been trying to find the right time to tell you, but the longer I waited, the harder it became." He had a look of sincerity in his eyes.

Sequoia sat up in bed and squeezed his hand. "Sean, it's okay, whatever it is you can go ahead and tell me." "We have been through a lot these last several months, and we agreed to leave the past behind, but I couldn't." He rubbed his forehead before he continued. "There was this one girl I became kind of serious with a couple years ago. Her name was Sam. Then out of the blues she ended things with me. At the time I didn't care that much to find out why she did it, I just moved on. However, everything that happened with Sophia sparked a curiosity. I reached out to her, and it took some convincing, but she finally told me why she ended things."

"Sean...." she said in a whisper as she shared his sentiments. "Apparently Sophia had threatened her into ending things with me. Sophia had evidence of Sam paying off a police commissioner, for covering up a hit and run her brother did some time ago." "Wow! Sean that's---"

"I know, all along Sophia had been meddling in my life and I was blind to everything." "Her obsession for you was relentless. She has some serious psyche issues, and I am glad it has finally come to light.

Sean don't ever blame yourself for the decisions she made. You did nothing wrong."

She hugged him briefly before kissing him on his cheek. "Thank you, Sequoia It means a lot to me." "You're welcome my darling. Now let's get some sleep." "Yes, we definitely should. I need you to be well rested for your early morning workout." Sean gave her a seductive wink. She laughed. "That won't be a problem, as long as you don't call a time-out again." "I will never live down that one, will I?" he said as he joined in the laughter. "Nope, you never will!" She said, giving him a passionate kiss.

****

Ten years had passed since Sequoia took a leap at love, despite her insecurities and troubled past. Now here she was with the love of her life. Sequoia and Sean stood by Sequoia's mother's graveside in silence. It was her mother's birthday and every year, Sean made sure that they went to pay their respects.

After she laid the flowers and said a few words, they walked towards the waiting car. As they approached the car, their two children ran out to greet them... Zachary and Ziadie. They were twins, both six years old. "I am really considering if we should take them to New York with us to Marge's birthday party," Sequoia said as she tickled Zachary's side. Marge had suffered a stroke a couple of years ago after her husband died. Since she lived alone with no one to care for her, she and Sean made sure to finance her treatment by hiring a live-in nurse to take care of her. "Yeah, me too," he said as he tried to move an energetic Ziadie from between his legs. "You sure you don't want Ms. Pam to come with us and help out?" "No, we will be fine. We've got this," she chuckled. "I hope you're right."

Sequoia was excited to attend the surprise party. Tessa and Todd, along with their three kids would be there, as well as Tiffany and her husband. She had not seen them in years, even though they stayed in touch. She knew that Marge was going to be elated at this surprise to see them all together again. She even invited Lucy, who had become a great confidante in her life. She too was married with two kids.

As they drove home to their beautiful home in the hills, Sequoia could not help but smile to herself. Never had she thought she would have a life like this, where she was a biochemist, a mother of two children and have a great and supportive husband. That year, following all the events that transpired, was one of the toughest years for them both. They had to deal with court meetings concerning Sophia's trial for the murder of Ashley, as well as dealing with the media. It was not easy, especially after they found out Sophia had hired a hit man while she was in jail to kill Sequoia. It was one of the most terrifying moments in her life… she almost died. She began to remember her stiff body on the ground as she bled out. The hit man stood over her with his gun aimed at her head, after he spent several minutes torturing her — Sophia's request. She thought it was the end of her life, so she closed her eyes to avoid seeing her death but after she heard the gunshots, it was not her body that lay lifeless on the ground. She looked up through her blood-stained vision to see Sean coming towards her with tear-filled eyes. He had shot the hit man twelve times! When she was transferred to the hospital, she had to get four different surgeries done, with several months of rehab and counseling. Sean and Marge stood by her side every moment of every day until she was better. Sean wasted no time in relocating her to California where their life finally began. "Mom, can we get Aunt Marge a gift at the store before we go?" Zadie's sweet innocent voice snapped her back into reality. "Sure, we can honey." A last thought crossed her mind before she returned to reality. "Sean?" "Yes dear?" "I have been meaning to ask you this for several years now, but I kept forgetting." He laughed.

"The fact that it's been several years, and you keep forgetting, makes me wonder if you should still be asking." She laughed and gave him a playful nudge. "Whatever... better late than never! Anyways, after that first weekend we spent together at your cabin, I had an unexpected surprise." He turned to her and asked.

"And what was that surprise?" "A loan company I had applied to a few years back had denied my loan application, but somehow after that weekend together, I received an email where they had approved my loan. And the amount was much more than I had applied for. Did you happen to have anything to do with that by chance?" He had a smirk on his face as he blushed. "I knew you would not have taken any help from me in that kind of way, so I improvised." She laughed. "I had a feeling it was you but I always thought you would have confessed on your own." "What can I say? I am good at keeping secrets." Then he gave her a wink.

She gave him a warm smile and nodded her head in approval. "Mom, Dad look!" Ziadie said in excitement as she pointed to several butterflies hovering around the fountain at their driveway. As soon as the car stopped, both children ran out of the car in excitement to admire the butterflies.

Sequoia and Sean joined them. A butterfly flew directly onto Sequoia's hand and tickled her. She held her hand up as she stared at the insect in admiration. It looked exactly like the butterfly in her dream that she had a few years ago of her mother. She smiled to herself at the coincidence. "Beautiful creatures aren't they, hun?" Sean asked. "Yes, they are," she replied and smiled to herself. Sequoia learned a lot those past few years and she knew she had overcome one of her greatest fears... the feeling of being worthy of love despite her past.

THE END

ABOUT THE AUTHOR

Antonett Clarke grew up in Jamaica where she started her journey as a Registered Nurse, but she always had a passion for writing since she was nine years old. She wrote fictional stories of all genres and like her first book, it integrates some of life's challenges that most people face at some point in their life.

Now residing in the United States, she delights in spending time with her family, writing stories while working as a full-time nurse. She hopes to share her stories with people from all walks of life and to eventually branch out into screen writing.

Stay connected because more books will drop soon. Also, please send me a review by either tagging me on social media or emailing antonett_clarke28@yahoo.com

www.ingramcontent.com/pod-product-compliance
Lightning Source LLC
Chambersburg PA
CBHW051526050726
47503CB00014B/1981